For Karen xx

~ DIVINE ~

Suz Korb

Copyright © 2021 Suz Korb. All rights reserved.
suzkorb.com
First published in Great Britain in 2013 by Suz Korb. This edition published in Great Britain in 2021 by Ink Hills.

No part of this publication may be reproduced, distributed, or transmitted in any form or by any means, including photocopying, recording, or other electronic or mechanical methods, without the prior written permission of the publisher, except in the case of brief quotations embodied in critical reviews and certain other noncommercial uses permitted by copyright law. For permission requests contact the publisher: inkhills@gmail.com with "permission request" in the subject field.

Any references to historical events, real people, real places, or real circumstances, are used fictitiously. Names, characters, places, and circumstances are products of the author's imagination. This book is sold subject to the condition that it shall not, by way of trade or otherwise, be lent, resold, hired out, or otherwise circulated without the publisher's prior consent in any form of binding or cover other than that in which it is published and without a similar condition, including this condition, being imposed on the subsequent purchaser.

Ink Hills supports the environment by utilizing Print on Demand publishing where your own unique copy of any of our paperback books are printed specifically for you when you order, on a one-off basis. We also first and foremost supply ebooks and audiobooks with a zero carbon footprint. Ink Hills POD paper books are supplied by Amazon KDP which utilizes sustainable forest paper but is currently not FSC certified officially, due to international supply management.

PRAISE ON AMAZON FOR
DIVINE
~ STORIES ONE TO FIVE ~

"A joy to read."
B. Robinson

"I really enjoyed reading the collection of stories in this book. They each flowed beautifully and I loved the simplicity of the characters and the backgrounds. It made the stories really easy to follow. I will definitely look forward to reading more from this author."
Raven

"An easy read and it kept me engaged."
Becky11

"Fast paced and interesting. Easy to read fun."
Mrs LS Smith

ALSO BY
~ SUZ KORB ~

THE BEDEVILED TRILOGY
Eve Eden vs the Zombie Horde
Eve Eden vs the Blood Sucking Vampires
Eve Eden vs the Devilish Demon

THE SUPERDUPER SERIES
Superstellar
Superpower

COMING OF AGE
Jude
That Night

TEEN ADVENTURE NOVELS
The Keystone
Flutterby

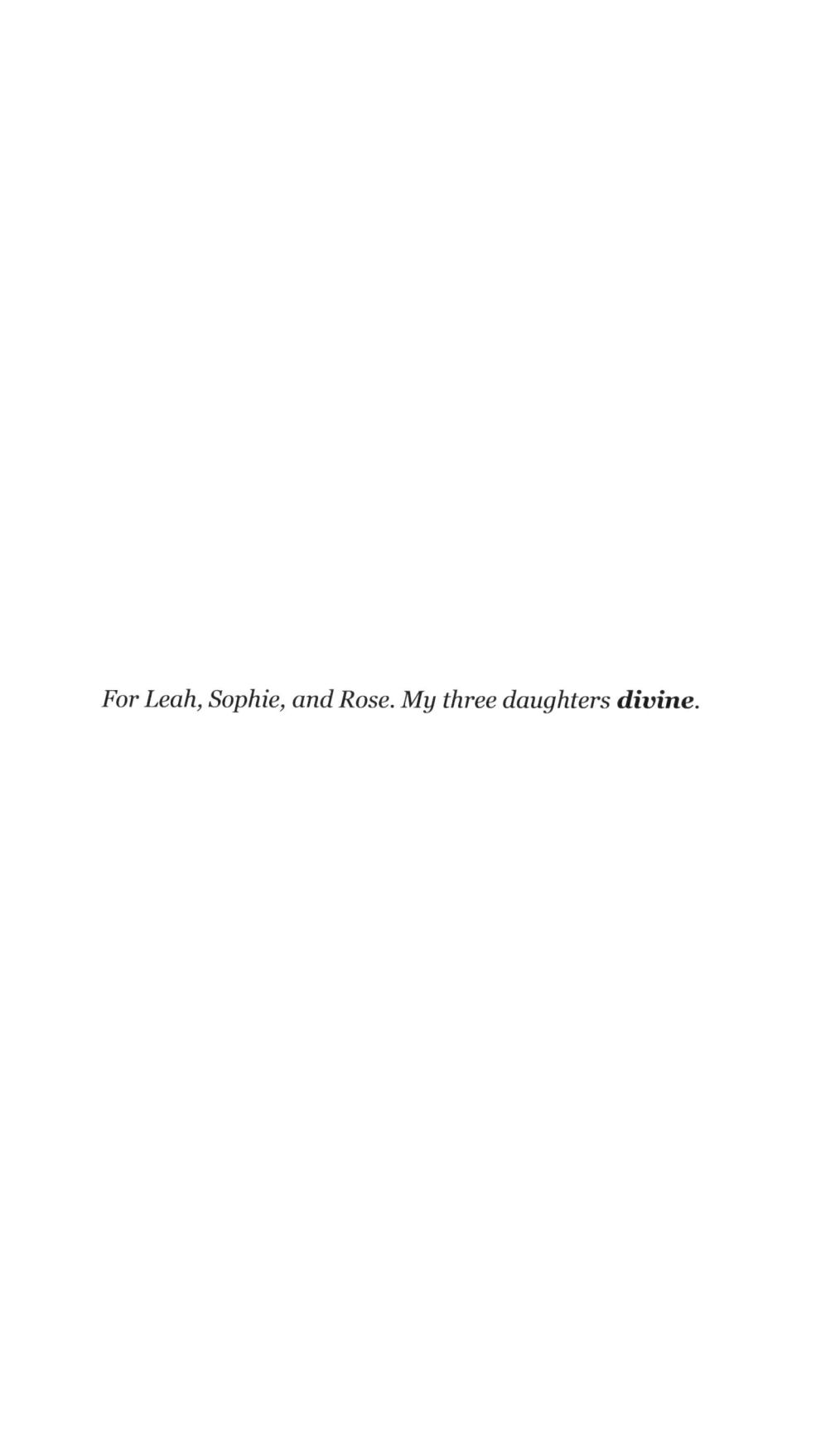

*For Leah, Sophie, and Rose. My three daughters **divine**.*

CONTENTS

Death by Chocolate	1
Dating a God	57
Gorgon Cursed	99
Rock Star	144
Dream Come True	182
About the Author	235

~ STORY ONE ~

~ Death by Chocolate ~

My alarm clock goes off with a dream-shredding blare. Sitting straight up in bed, I must not lie down again or I'll fall back asleep in a heartbeat. I jam my hand down onto the alarm clock and my awakened nerves relax when the annoying buzzing sound stops.

I'm shaken.

My whole body won't stop quivering as an after effect of being ripped from my dreams. And what a dream it was. I've never dreamed like that before. The place where my mind was during its dream-state was so… so…

Powerful.

A powerful dream place. A powerful notion.

"Weird," I say aloud.

I stretch my arms and legs. My shivers have died down. I toy with the ends of my long dark hair before getting out of bed. Padding my way sleepily across the carpet, I exit my bedroom and head straight into the basement bathroom. When I get into said bathroom I practically stuff my whole face into the sink and start brushing my teeth. When I finally lift my head and gaze into the mirror I stop brushing immediately.

Staring back at me in the reflection are two extra heads.

Now comes the screaming. I just can't help myself. Seeing two extra heads upon my shoulders is enough to make gurgling sounds ooze out of the back of my throat.

I scream and scream some more. My toothbrush is poised in the air. Arm bent, elbow out. Toothpaste foam surrounds my lips and a blob of minty froth drips off my chin. I don't hear it plop into the sink because I'm still too busy screaming.

The extra head on my left shoulder is a woman's. A woman's head with blonde hair that's trailing down *my* arm. My own head is obviously between my shoulders where it's supposed to be and on my right shoulder is the head of Santa Claus; complete with fluffy white beard.

Despite the fact that my own mouth is in the shape of a huge O, the mouths of the extra heads are moving. I think they are speaking. I'd probably be able to hear them if I could stop screaming.

This situation is far too traumatic for my poor little mind, which snaps, and I pass out.

*

I wake up on the floor of my bathroom with no idea how I got here. Some dream about two extra heads niggles at the back of my mind. My hands brush my shoulders, but when I don't feel anything but collarbone, I brush the thought aside and balk at my own silliness. Then, I stand and hop into the shower.

After scrubbing myself clean under super-hot water I dry off with a towel and zoom out of the bathroom without looking into the mirror. Once in my bedroom I get dressed in a hurry and run upstairs. I gulp down a bowl of cereal for breakfast and then I zoom out the front door. I'm on my way to Lakepoint High. I'm a Senior, I'm seventeen years old and I've got tons to do today. I don't know how I'd managed to fall asleep on the bathroom floor earlier and the fact that I did means I'm going to be at least twenty minutes late for first period.

*

The class I was late for has now ended and I've just met up with my best friend, Shana.

"Kate." She says my name and flicks her blonde hair over her shoulder. "Did you get Mandy's text message?"

We've made it to our shared locker. I dial the combination, open the steel door and chuck my bookbag inside. "What message?"

"Mandy said she's sick so she can't make the cake for tonight's fundraiser."

I feel like the floor has just gone out from under me. I'm disappointed in Mandy and now I'm extremely panicked, because I don't know who is going to make the cake.

"She's sick?" I reach into our locker and grab my cell off the top shelf. When I turn it on a message pings onto the screen. Sure enough, there's a text from Mandy saying she has the flu.

"Who gets the flu in summer?" I ask Shana rhetorically. "Now who's going to make the Death by Chocolate Cake?"

"Don't worry, Kate." Shana pushes me aside so she can fix her lipgloss in the tiny mirror that's stuck to the inside of the locker door. A mirror which I am highly avoiding looking into for some unknown reason. "We can make the cake."

"Oh my gosh, no we can't," I mumble.

Shana bangs the locker door shut and we both traipse down the hall. "Don't you remember what happened the last time we tried to bake cupcakes?" I'm desperately trying to talk some sense into her now.

"Well, Mandy's the one who always says a chef should improvise."

"Yeah, but not by leaving out the flour." I'm incredulous that she can't seem to remember the consistency of our attempted cupcakes. "Those cupcakes we made could have been used as erasers."

Shana giggles.

I round on her as we stop in front of the doorway to the classroom. "How can you laugh at a time like this?" Cell phone still in hand, I shake it a little threateningly in front of her face. "I'm in charge of this fundraiser event tonight and it's totally going to get screwed up now."

"Chill out, Kate." Shana knocks my phone aside. "I didn't laugh."

She didn't?

I look at my phone, wondering if there's a call on it. Its screen is blank though and when I next look up Shana has already disappeared into the classroom. I could have sworn I heard her laugh when she was standing at my left. As I make my way down the hall I've got a strange feeling about the sound of that laugh.

It came from the vicinity of my left shoulder.

*

I meet Shana again after school. Together, we head to the grocery store to pick up ingredients for the cake we're going to have to make. We're down the baking aisle and I'm just about to grab a bag of flour off the shelf when Shana slaps the back of my hand.

"Ouch," I hiss. "What did you do that for?"

"We don't need flour."

"Um, hello?" I'm weirded out by her baking tactics and lack of a sensible memory. "Rubber cupcakes, remember?"

"That's because we tried to cook those." Shana drags me by the hand further down the aisle. "Today we have everything we need right here." She indicates the shelves of ready-made cakes and containers of frosting. "We'll just get a cake and pour a million layers of different chocolate stuff on top."

"But that's cheating."

"No one will ever know." She whispers conspiratorially.

"We'll know." A man's voice says.

I fling my head to the right. We're busted. Someone from school has overheard our conversation and now the whole fundraiser will be ruined.

No one's there.

I turn around and around, searching in every direction for the source of that voice I know I'd heard.

"What are you doing, Kate?" Shana grabs my shoulders and turns me around to face her. "This is no time for practicing dance routines." She releases me and starts piling cake frosting and other chocolate goodies into her basket. "We've got a cake to slam together and it has to be so chocolaty that if anyone takes a single bite of it they'll die from chocolate overdose."

When I don't respond to her obvious hyperbole, she stops gathering supplies.

"Are you okay?"

Her question alarms me. *Am* I okay? I don't know. Do people who are okay hear voices inside their heads?

"Oh my gosh, it's him." Shana is no longer concerned with my well-being. She's too busy looking over my shoulder. When I turn around I see the person in question she's *oh-my-goshing* about.

It's Jason. Jason Fulmen is heading toward us. His long-ish blonde hair twists naturally to the side a little.

I've always wanted Jason. I mean, I've always wanted to *meet* Jason. Stupid brain, making me think I *want* him. I'm so noodle-minded today.

"He's weird." Shana comments as he nears.

"He's not weird," I reply. "He's just shy."

It's true. Ever since Jason arrived at Lakepoint High in Sophomore year, he's been a shy guy. A totally hot shy guy. Every girl has tried to get to know him and each one has suffered a *mega fail* in the asking-him-out department. He hasn't dated anyone.

"I think he's gay."

I shove Shana in the shoulder for saying this. "Would it matter if he was?"

"No, but you'd be disappointed…"

Her voice trails off as Jason nears. "Are you still bringing some chocolate to the fundraiser tonight, Jason?"

He takes something off the shelf as Shana strides over to him. He turns and looks at her and then past her at me.

Actually, he's not just looking at me, he's now gaping. His jaw is dropped open. He looks astonished. His blue eyes are wide and they dart back and forth.

He backs away.

"Where are you going?" Shana asks him. She turns around to face me and silently mouths the word "weirdo". By the time she turns back around he's gone.

"Told you that guy is weird."

I walk toward Shana. "At least he agreed to help with the fundraiser." I think I partially agree with her about Jason being a little weird, because just before he'd left I could have sworn he'd been gawking at the sides of my head.

*

We're at the fundraiser. It's being held in the school auditorium. Shana had spoken with the tech guys and managed to get a chocolate display onto the big screen.

There's a huge chocolate fountain in the center of the room. Circled around the perimeter of the auditorium are tables with chocolate displays. Almost half the senior class pitched in and set up booths filled with treats, all in hopes of raising money for the school library.

Shana and I are in the middle. We've set up a table and roped off the circular fountain. If anyone wants to dip some strawberries into the flowing cocoa they'll have to pay a fee after lining up. Which they do. In droves. Everyone loves a chocolate fountain!

The event goes smoothly. People are enticed by the display of chocolates on the big screen. I haven't had a single bite of chocolate all night though. I haven't even dipped into the *fontaine au chocolat*.

"Aren't you going to indulge, Kate?"

Shana, on the other hand, has been gobbling sweets all night.

"The choc is supposed to be bought," I say in response to her question.

She licks her fingers and looks up at the huge chocolate fountain. "We're not exactly in danger of running out of chocolate."

"You're going to make yourself sick."

She scowls at me. "Don't be crazy, everyone knows chocolate is way good for you."

"Uh," I mumble. "Not *that* much chocolate. Seriously, slow down."

"I'll slow down after I've tried our cake."

Wow. After all the chocolate she's already eaten Shana actually dares to eat some of the diabolical cake we made? There isn't one single layer within that cake that isn't chocolate.

Earlier this afternoon, when we'd first looked at all the ingredients we'd bought, we'd decided the cake pan we'd purchased was too small. We were at Shana's house and she'd ended up putting all the ingredients into a giant punch bowl.

The Death by Chocolate Cake is sitting almost menacingly on the table in front of us now. I can see every chocolaty layer of it through the glass of the bowl. On the bottom is the actual chocolate cake we'd bought, not baked. The next layer on top of that is chocolate frosting, then a layer of chocolate chips and so on.

What we've got here is a death wish in a bowl. It's a good thing the so-called "cake" isn't being sold to just one person. If we served more than one bite per customer, it could send the eater into some kind of sugar coma.

The fundraiser slows down. There are only about thirty people left in the auditorium. No one has purchased a single scoop of the Death by Chocolate Cake and I don't blame them.

"I guess we wasted our time making this," I say, peeling off the plastic wrap from the punch bowl. "Mandy was going to make a real chocolate cake. This thing is just a mess. I'm going to trash it when I get home."

"Oh no you're not."

I look up. Standing in front of me is a tall man with curly hair. "I'll have some of that cake please."

Well, well. Surprise, surprise. So someone does want to eat some of this "interesting" cake after all.

Actually, a lot of people are suddenly interested in the Death by Chocolate Cake.

Shana gladly starts scooping out massive portions of the cake to customers. Soon, everyone in the auditorium has wandered over and been served with a slice (more like blob) of dark oozing sugar.

Well, everyone except for one person.

I notice Jason is standing behind his table that's loaded with chocolate. I'm surprised he'd agreed to help out with the fundraiser. I guess he must have talked to Shana about it weeks ago, because I definitely didn't invite him. Not that I hadn't thought about inviting him, I'd just thought he would have ignored me or something.

He's certainly not ignoring me now. He keeps eyeballing me with a strange expression on his face before looking quickly away once again.

People start eating cake. Including Shana. When she catches me staring at her she reaches into the pocket of her jeans, pulls out what I assume is $2.00 in change, and adds it to the money pot.

"Happy now?"

I think that's what she just said. Her mouth is stuffed with chocolate so her words come out sounding like: "hoopah nah?"

"Whatever makes you happy, Shana." I watch her eat. Chocolate definitely makes her happy. Lots and lots of chocolate.

She takes yet another bite of the chocolate goo. "Mmmmm," she says delectably. "Ooh," she mumbles not-so-deliciously.

Shana puts her plate of chocolate mess down and rubs her tummy. "I think I ate too much." She states the obvious.

I don't even bother with the I-told-you-sos. She's going to have a serious sugar hangover in the morning. No need for me to add to her impending discomfort.

"Ooh," someone else moans.

"Eww."

"Argh."

"Ouch." One little girl, who is about six years old, is rubbing her tummy. "My belly hurts." She looks up and complains to a woman who I assume is her mother.

Uh oh. I'm starting to think the cake we made is about to live up to its name. Everyone who has eaten it is complaining.

"What are the ingredients of this cake?" The little girl's mom is talking to me now. Actually, a lot of people are talking to me. They're all demanding I tell them our secret recipe.

"Argh!" Someone screams from the back of the crowd. There's a thumping noise and then someone else bellows. Soon there are more thumping sounds and I realize I'm hearing the noise of people going down.

One by one they fall until everyone in the room is on the floor.

The cake we'd made has lived up to its name; our Death by Chocolate Masterpiece has killed everyone at this event.

I fall down too, even though I haven't been cake poisoned, I'm just distraught and I need to get to my fallen friend. I crawl on my knees toward Shana who's lying on the floor. I start to shake her by the shoulders, begging her to wake up. When she's unresponsive I check for a breath.

She's not breathing!

I've poisoned my best friend!

Immediately, I place my hands one on top of the other, onto her chest. I'd learned CPR last year, so I know exactly what to do. I start pumping her heart and I only stop briefly to reach into my pocket and pull out my cell. I punch the numbers into the screen and I'm about to make the call.

Whoosh!

My phone goes flying from my hand of its own accord as though attached to an invisible string. It hits a pair of standing legs and crashes to the floor, smashing into pieces of battery and plastic cover.

"What the...?" I shout. My phone had crashed into Jason's legs. He ignores the pieces of my phone and walks swiftly toward me, stepping over prone bodies.

"Jason!" I screech his name. "I don't know what's happening here, please help me!" My voice trembles because I've started to cry.

Tears stream down my face. "I've killed all these people with my poisonous cake!"

"They're not dead, Kate."

I'm momentarily shocked that Jason knows my name. That thought barely flits across my consciousness though, I'm a lot more concerned with the other thing he just said.

"What do you mean, they're not dead?" I shriek. "Look at them!"

"Yes, Kate," Jason says. He gets to his knees at the same time I stand up. "Look and see."

Why is he talking like that? And why is he so calm when there is so much death all around us? Most importantly, what is he doing to Shana's forehead?

I don't have time to react and shove him away from my best friend. Something erupts out of the place where Jason is touching Shana and it's even weirder than when my phone had magically flown out of my hand.

An opaque glass floor is spreading out beneath Jason's palm. I squeak in astonishment and cover my mouth with my hand. "What's happening?" I whisper behind tears of confusion.

The illusion of glass emanates outward so that when I look down it seems as though I'm standing in a pool that comes up to my shins. The whole of the auditorium floor is soon layered upon by a strange sheet of glass. Under it, I can see all the prostrate bodies.

"What did you do?" I squeak again at Jason from behind my hand.

"You can see this, can't you?" He answers my question with a question and then he stands up.

The second he breaks contact with Shana's forehead, the glass floor vanishes.

"What was that?" I've dropped my hand and I'm backing away because Jason is coming toward me.

"I'll show you exactly what that was, Kate." He reaches out to me. I cringe and back away even further until I bump into the edge of the table.

"She has to go now, son." A woman's voice penetrates deep into my left ear hole. I whip my head to the side.

"Who said that?"

"Take her there." A man's voice booms into my right ear at the same time I'd started speaking.

"What's going on?" I cry out after turning my head to the right and finding no one there.

"I'm really sorry about this, Kate." Jason is right in front of me "We have to go now."

Go? Go where? What in the he–

My internal question doesn't get asked. Jason grabs my hand and the same sheet of opaque glass explodes in front of my eyes. All I now know is shards of what was once consciousness.

*

Actually, I hadn't fallen asleep, nor had I gotten knocked out or even faint.

When the glassy vision recedes, I find it's now under my feet. It's as though I'm staring at a bathroom window, like the ones that are slightly frosted so that you can't see any naked showering persons inside.

That fuzzy glass is gone from the space in front of my eyes and it's now the surface I'm standing on.

For miles and miles in every direction I'm standing on this strange glassy surface. The sky above is gray, dull and so lifeless I don't know if it's an actual sky or a ceiling. Whatever it is, it seems to press down on me like a weight of emotional depression.

I collapse and almost fall all the way onto the glassy ground. My butt doesn't make contact with the strange surface though. Instead, I'm crumpled up hugging my knees and my ankles are taking my weight as I rest on them and rock back and forth.

"Where am I?" I mumble as my mind sizzles with uncertainty.

"You're in Hades land. We all are."

"Who said that?" I stand back up and whirl around.

I'm face to face with Jason. He's standing on the glass ground and he's no longer dressed in jeans and a t-shirt.

From shoulders to mid-thigh, he's covered in an elaborately wrapped curtain. The fabric is a light blue and bound at the waist with a fancily braided silver belt. Come to think of it, he has silver all over him. He's got swirling arm and ankle bands and his feet are encased in gladiator sandals.

"What the heck are you wearing?" I screech at the top of my lungs. I don't actually care about his stupid toga ensemble because I'm hysterical with worry about where I am, so it's the first question that had popped out of my mouth.

Jason sighs. "I'm wearing the cloth of the gods, just like you are, Kate."

I look down at myself when he says this.

He wasn't kidding. I'm dressed in the same style he is. I'm dressed like an idiot from back in time, or better yet, another planet! For all I know we could *be* on another planet.

I'm wearing flowing robes. That is, yards and yards of deep red cloth flow from an empire waistline down to my ankles. All the fabric I'm clothed in is done up in gold swirls that clasp the material elaborately upon my shoulders.

"What's going on with my hair?" I touch my hair and my hand practically bounces back. I think my locks are up in curls and I definitely have no idea how it could have become styled in such a way.

"I don't feel so good." My hands aren't concerned with my hair now, they're both clasped to my belly. I double over and my knees hit the ground. "Where are we?"

Panic starts to set in. I can barely see the strange surface beneath me through my tears. The blurry vision takes on a familiar shape that rocks me to my core.

"I told you, we're in Hades' land, Kate... the Underworld."

Jason says this at the same time I lower my face even closer to the ground. At first I think I detect a reflection in the glassy surface. It is a face I'm staring at but it isn't my own. Actually, there are a lot of faces. The one staring directly back at me is a face I know.

It's Shana's face. She's underneath the very glass I'm kneeling on.

"Shana!" I wail and start pounding at the opaque surface. "Shana! Can you hear me?"

I don't even care about the other faces I can see below right now. All I care about is how my best friend got in there and how exactly I'm going to get her out.

"I don't think that's going to work, Kate." Jason places his hand on my shoulder. I stop pounding on the glassy ground and look up at him.

I stand and wipe tears from my eyes. "Well what am I supposed to do?"

"We don't know."

We? "So why did you stop me then? Help me crack this glass!" I indicate the ground below. "We need to get Shana out of there!"

"Mother? Father?"

"Who are you talking to?"

"I'll show you." Jason opens his hand. It's empty for a second and then silver mirror is lying in his palm.

I'm spooked. "How did you do that?" I gasp. He holds it up and I gaze at my reflection. It's the same reflection I saw in my bathroom mirror this morning.

It's me with two extra heads.

I begin to hyperventilate and I fall to the ground. The skirt of the red fabric I'm wearing pools out all around me, puffing up so that I have to punch it back down in frustration. "This isn't happening," I whisper. I glare at Shana's faded face beneath the foggy surface below. I look all around me and I notice more faces beneath the glassy ground.

"It's definitely happening, Kate." Jason sits next to me. He's holding that stupid mirror up to my face again. "My parents wouldn't just attach themselves to anyone's shoulders, you know."

I look up from the ground as he speaks. I don't really know if I'm listening properly because I'm too busy gaping in astonishment at my reflection.

"Santa and a blonde bombshell woman are your parents?" I blurt. "Get them off me!"

Jason laughs. He actually chuckles during this diabolical situation. My gaze goes from the mirror to his face. His smile is almost more mesmerizing than the sight of two extra heads staring back at me from atop my shoulders.

I blink. My mind is awhirl. I look from Jason's extremely good looking face, to the faces I see in the mirror, and down at the faces under the ground.

Faces everywhere. My eyes can't take it all in. I'm experiencing visual sensory overload and it's enough to make me dizzy. I think Jason is talking to me again. I'm not sure though, because upon the horizon a moving glass city has just arisen.

"What the hell is that?"

I didn't yell that just now, both the voices at the sides of my head did.

I jump to my feet and Jason stands up too. He whirls around and faces the oncoming city. I am so not kidding here. There are towers of glass in the distance, all crammed together like buildings.

"That is a moving city, of course," I say to the heads that I know rest upon my shoulders. "What else could it be?" I've decided I lost my mind a long time ago, so why not describe what it is I'm actually seeing?

"Let's get out of here!" Jason shouts, turns back around and grabs my hand.

"I'm not leaving Shana!" I yell back at him and I wrench my hand from his. Jason stops and rounds on me. The sound of the approaching glass city is incredible. It's rumbling steadily toward us and soon enough I can't hear the protestations coming out of Jason's mouth. Even if this is all some kind of crazy nightmare, I'm not about to abandon my best friend to the oncoming buildings.

I kneel down. The ground rumbles as I start pounding my fists onto it once again.

"That won't work, you foolish girl!" Over the cacophony that is the moving glass city, I can hear the head on my left shoulder screaming into my ear.

Crack.

The glass finally splits beneath my fist.

"How did she do that?" The sound of Santa's voice booms into my right earhole.

I've made a dent in the ground. Jason is now bent down beside me as I strike at the glass surface.

Many cracks appear and widen. The glass encasing Shana opens up. The rumbling city nears. Jason and I back away and below me, Shana's body is now exposed. Her eyes blink and I lean over and grasp her hand.

"Shana!" I scream. "Get up right now!"

She doesn't need telling twice. Shana's grip tightens around my hand and I pull her out of the translucent ground.

There's a split second in which all three of us stand there gaping at the rising glass city. We are mere specs down here below its approaching grandeur. I've still got hold of Shana's hand and Jason grabs my other.

Together, we turn and run.

"We're DOOMED!"

The second word Jason just said is very loud because the crashing noise of the moving glass city has stopped. We're all still running and I glance back.

"Look!" I shout and halt my footsteps. Jason's hand flies out of mine and so does Shana's.

We all turn around and gape at the nearby city which is no longer a moving one.

Tall spires of multi-colored glass shoot up everywhere from the ground. Each glassy building is not transparent and only some have see-through windows.

"What is that?" Shana wails. "Where the hell are we?"

"That's exactly where we are." Jason is gasping and I think he's a little out of breath.

I open my mouth to reply at the same time a low reverberating sound comes from the base of the city. It looks as though the glass buildings sprout right up out of the ground. The bottom of every building is one great opaque glass wall. A wall that is cracking open until a piece of it moves aside like a door.

Out of this door spills people. Lots and lots of people. Men, women and children all march toward us in neat rows.

"Who are they?"

I shrug my shoulders and I'm surprised when this act is easy. I don't feel like I've got two extra heads. When they both start talking though, I realize I do. And I want them gone.

"This doesn't bode well," Santa says.

Bode?

"No, it does not." The blonde head chimes into my ear.

"What does bode mean?" I say, rounding on Jason. He looks at me, quizzically. "Santa said *bode* and I'm confused."

"*You're* confused?" Shana replies to me with tears in her eyes. "You just pulled me out of the ground and you're talking about being confused about a word?"

"Santa?" Jason says.

"Yeah, you know, this head?" I point at my right shoulder.

"Head?" Shana glowers at me. "What head?"

"Oh, you mean the human fantasy of Kris Kringle?" Jason moves forward and grabs my hand once again. He also takes Shana's hand and urges us both away. "That's not Santa, Kate." As we all move quickly over the glass ground, he attempts an explanation. "I told you, that's my father Zeus and my mother Hera. I'm their youngest son. I was born only seventeen years ago."

Telling me his family history doesn't make a whole lot more sense and I'm still not convinced the white bearded guy isn't Santa.

"Oh no!" Shana screams as I'm hit from behind by a blunt object. As I fall, I notice she and Jason do too. The crowd at our backs wasn't as far away as I'd thought. Also, they've just attacked.

*

We're carried by the throngs of people into the glass city. There is much protestation by screaming on our part that none of these people are listening to.

I can't see my surroundings until we're each unceremoniously dumped onto the glassy ground. The crowd of people back away and Shana, Jason and I are sitting in a vast open space. All around us are the tall glass buildings beyond the crowd.

"My parents' heads are gone," Jason whispers.

I look at him, curious. Is he saying he can't see my two extra heads any longer? This could be cause for celebration, despite being trapped in this weird environment.

"Pssst."

I look to my right and left, wondering if that noise was one of my two extra heads, after all.

"Pssst."

Nope. That sound came from directly behind. I turn at the same time Shana and Jason do.

"You three better hide," a young male voice says. I squint my eyes and look deep into the crowd. All I see are still standing bodies with expressionless faces staring back at me. Actually, everyone seems to be staring vacantly. Their eyes are open, but no man, woman or child seems to be focusing on anything. They're all wearing regular twenty-first century clothing.

A guy peeks his head around from behind a rather large bodied woman. "Get over here," he says urgently.

I look from Shana to Jason. Shana shrugs her shoulders while Jason nods his head. All three of us get to our feet. We scramble into the crowd. It's a tight squeeze but eventually all the bodies shift. Like each particle in the universe Shana, Jason and I fall naturally into place in a sifted crowd.

I look at the person who urged us over. He's dressed like me and Jason.

Shana snorts a laugh. She's allowed. She's wearing her own clothing of jeans and a t-shirt.

"What's so funny?" The guy asks her. He picks up the hem of his skirt and gives it a little flick. "Don't you like my dress?"

I grin wide when he smiles and Shana giggles.

"I've been wearing this since I got here," he says. "I have no idea where I am and I have no idea why I'm dressed like this." His hair is dark and cut short. His eyes are green, not blue like Jason's. Not that I'm comparing the two guys. If I was though, I'd say they're almost the same height, like six feet or something. I'd also say he's about seventeen years old, like us.

His dress comes to mid-thigh although it's not quite as elaborately decorated with silver like Jason's short robes. The guy's get-up is made of dark brown leather with metal clasps here and there.

He kind of looks like a gladiator.

"I was going to ask when you changed," Shana says to me. "I guess you can wear anything in a dream."

"Yep." The guy sticks out his hand. "I'm Dillon," he says.

"Welcome to my dream."

I take his hand and give it a quick shake. "Hi Dillon. I'm Kate and this is Shana and Jason who are part of *my* dream."

"You got my name right." Shana steps a little closer. "But this whole place is my nightmare."

"If you all think you're dreaming then why did you bother hiding?" Jason throws up his hands in disgust.

"To see where my subconscious takes me on this weird adventure, of course." Shana eyeballs our outfits some more. "I'll prove it's my dream. Watch." She scrunches up her face in concentration. When nothing else happens to her for a few seconds, she opens her eyes.

"What are you doing?" I ask her.

"I was trying to zap myself into a dress like yours, Kate."

"Why would you want to be dressed like this, even in your worst nightmare?" I give my long skirts a twirl. "And my hair is hideous." I shake my head and my curls bounce around.

"Hmmm." Shana puts a finger to her pursed lips. "I always heard that if you're dreaming and you realize it, you can control what happens."

"NONE OF YOU ARE DREAMING!" Jason booms.

"Sssshhhhhh!" Dillon hisses.

Rumble, rumble goes the ground.

"It's happening." Dillon freezes. He stands still and faces directly forward. "Get in line and don't move."

"What? Why?" I say, over the escalating rumbling noises.

"Ssshhhhhh!" Dillon shushes me again and we obey. He's obviously been here longer than any of us have. The panic in his voice makes me wonder if all this really isn't a dream.

I haven't heard anything from either of my two extra heads, so

I'm wondering if they truly are gone from my shoulders.

The rumbling stops. Shana and Jason go rigid and I follow suit. We all stare straight ahead.

Through the crowd I can see into the clearing. Well, the space we'd been carried into *used* to be clear. Now there are prostrate bodies lying on the glass surface. They're spread out and I'd say it's a group of about thirty people. Women, children and men of varying ages. Just like the members of the crowd I'm immersed in.

A hissing sound builds and I'm wondering if Dillon is shushing me again.

He isn't.

In a swirl of misty smoke and light, a woman appears in the clearing, hovering above the ground. I almost cry out in astonishment. I hold my breath instead and I don't squeak a single word.

The floating woman's bare feet touch the ground as the light gray fog around her dissipates. She's wearing long, flowing robes of jet-black and she's even more decorated with swirls of silver than Jason and his silver-covered ensemble.

The woman has black hair too. It's woven through with strands of silver. She steps over and past the bodies on the ground. She lifts her arms in an arch like a choral conductor and the bodies rise.

The people are now standing. They look like they are awake except that their eyes are all unfocused like the members of the large crowd.

I recognize one of them. It's a little girl. The same girl from the fundraiser at Lakepoint High. I realize now that I recognize all their faces.

These are the people who'd eaten my deadly Death by Chocolate

Cake. Their faces are the ones I'd seen under the glassy ground, right before I'd dug Shana out. The moving city had roamed right over them and now here they stand. Faces still, yet haunted.

I risk a glance at Shana. Her face is a blank. I don't mean she doesn't have eyes, a nose and lips. I mean, her expression matches those of most of the people we're amongst.

A blank stare.

I look at Jason and Dillon. They're either faking it, or they too have become zombie-like in their demeanor.

I figure I'd better follow suit so I stare aimlessly ahead. As I do, the woman in black waves her arms again. When she does the people near her start to walk forward, they mingle into the larger gathering and I'm pushed back deeper into the masses. I can barely see ahead into the clearing now. I catch a glimpse of a new swirling accumulation. Black vapor coils near the woman. It coalesces into the shape of a man dressed in long, flowing white robes. He looks like an ancient Greek god and I'm starting to detect a theme. Whether or not this is a dream sequence I'm suffering, the hot topic seems to be an Olympian fantasy.

The black smoke fades and the man stands proud and tall. "You've done well, Persephone," he says to the black clad woman. "My army grows mightier by your expert hand."

An army. Oh great. I shudder to think what this means, because the crowd I'm standing in could definitely be described as some kind of soldier-gathering thing.

The woman he called Persephone kisses the man on the cheek. "Your master plan will succeed, Hades."

Hades? Now that name sounds familiar.

"Have you discovered any more halflings?"

"No."

Their conversation confuses me, because I can barely hear what they're saying, this far away.

"Then I'll proceed." This is the final thing I hear from Hades before I see him wave his arms. He holds them out in front of himself and something starts to happen to the crowd around me. Everyone starts putting out their own arms in the exact same manner Hades is. All their hands are fisted, so I quickly imitate them. I glace to my right and left. I can't see Shana, Jason or that Dillon guy anywhere.

I see Hades moving again. He steps forward and moves his arms into a protective X shape in front of his chest.

The crowd follows his exact movements and I force myself to do the same.

As Hades makes more strange moves, the reactions of the crowd speed up. Eventually everyone is kicking out and whirling their arms in arcs through the air. I'm struggling to keep up with the movements while trying to keep an eye on what Hades does next.

What he does do next is beyond my control. He tucks himself down into a ball.

I'm too late. By the time I start to dive down, Persephone has seen me. That's not all she sees either. I glimpse Jason and Dillon plummet to the floor at the same time as me.

"Halflings!" Persephone screeches.

I'm assuming Hades has stood up once again, because the people all around me have risen to their feet.

"Lie down." Hades voice booms and the crowd collapses.

I'm standing upright, fully exposed. Jason is stepping his way over bodies toward me and so is Dillon.

I don't know what to do. Should I lie down? Should I attempt to run away?

My eyes lock onto Hades'. He points at members of the crowd who stand. "Seize them!" He shouts. More and more bodies stand. They come between me, Jason and Dillon. I still haven't seen Shana anywhere. Hands lock around my arm and I'm positive I'm captured once again.

I'm whirled around by force and my eyes meet Dillon's. A golden swirl of fog surrounds us and everyone else disappears in a sparkling, misty haze.

Actually, it was Dillon and I who'd vanished.

I know this now because the golden smoke has cleared and we're standing on a cloud.

"Argh!" We both start screaming at the same time.

We are up in the air. We throw our arms around each other and squeeze. I also squeeze my eyes shut.

"Oh my gosh, oh my gosh, oh my gosh, what's happening?"

To say I'm panicked is an understatement of being-in-the-actual-atmosphere proportions.

"I think it's okay, Kate. Look."

"Nuh-uh." I say into his ear. I briefly wonder why I haven't heard either of my two heads say anything yet. That thought barely registers inside my addled mind for long though. If the extra heads are gone forever, I'm glad.

"Seriously, we're not falling."

I open my eyes halfway and I see a floating mountain in the distance, so I shut them again.

"Did you see that?" I whisper.

"What?"

"There's a flying mountain over there."

"Over where?"

"There!" I point straight ahead and then I realize I'm being stupid. I'm hugging this Dillon guy, so of course he can't see behind himself. Unless he can. It wouldn't surprise me if he could. Stranger things have happened in the last twenty-four hours than someone seeing out the back of their head.

I fling my eyes open and step back from Dillon. Placing my hands on his outer biceps, I immediately notice he's extremely buff. I turn him forcefully around and then I stand next to him.

"There," I say, pointing again.

"That mountain is floating!" Dillon shouts.

"Yes it... ARGH!" I scream when my eyes are drawn downwards. "It's... they are..."

Dillon turns. "That's what I was trying to tell you, Kate," he says urgently. "We're not falling."

"No, not that, look."

He follows my gaze downward, the cloud beneath our feet has thinned and we can both see the ground below.

It's the ground we just left. We are about a hundred feet above the glass city. From way up here I can see that it's a circle of buildings surrounding that great open space. I can see the crowd of people. I can see Hades and Persephone and I can also see that none of them are moving.

Everyone down there is standing stock still. Not moving a muscle.

"Why aren't they moving?" Dillon says the question I'd just been thinking.

"I don't know."

A feeling of deflation takes over and I have to sit down. My rear-end hits a soft surface. I can't tell if we're dangling up here, or if we're being supported by the thin clouds. Whatever the reason, the "surface" doesn't feel flat or even. It's all bumpy with soft, plump lumps like smooth… well… like clouds.

This sky isn't gray at all.

Dillon sits down next to me. "What's wrong, Kate? Never been cloud-sitting before?"

I look at him. Either this guy's sense of humor has terrible timing, or he's being serious and has done this kind of thing before.

"Um, no, I haven't."

"I was just kidding. Neither have I." He smiles at me. It brightens up his face. "It's not that bad up here, actually."

I look at him like he's lost his mind. I feel my forehead scrunch up in serious doubt for his sanity.

"I can see you might not agree." Dillon turns his head. "Just look at that, Kate. It's a floating island in the sky." He turns back around and looks down. "And that's where we used to be. It looks like they're stopped in time, or something. You don't get to see things like that every day, right?" His facial expression implores me.

I've only known this guy for a matter of minutes and I already like him. "Has anyone ever told you, you should be a floating-in-the-sky therapist?"

Dillon chuckles at my question.

"Thanks for calming me down."

"No problem." He smiles again. "Now what?"

"What?"

"What are we going to do? How do we get down from here."

His question exasperates me, because I obviously don't know the answer. I harrumph loudly and throw myself backward. My arms splay out and I sink into a cloud that's like a cushion. Tufts of foggy plumes poof up and out all around me.

The clouds below have thickened and we can't see the frozen people on the glassy ground anymore.

Dillon leans beside me on his elbow. I glare at the sky above as though I can *angry* it into letting us down from here.

"So tell me about yourself, Kate."

My gaze shifts to him. He wants to have a normal conversation up here in the sky. That's not normal at all. Then again, waking up with two extra heads and then being catapulted into a strange land with a glass ground isn't exactly normal either. What had Jason called that place down there? Hades land? The Underworld?

"I have two extra heads," I blurt.

Dillon nods his own head. "I think I believe you. After the week I've had I'm starting to think anything is possible."

I laugh.

"Damn, you're pretty when you smile." Dillon's face goes bright red. "I mean... not that you aren't pretty when you're not smiling." He shifts around uncomfortably on his cloud and my smile grows even wider. "Not that I'm like checking you out or anything..." He sits up and shakes his head. "I'm just going to shut up now."

I giggle and sit up too. "It's okay," I say, placing my hand on his shoulder. "I think your idea was great. We should get to know each other. Nothing else to do being stuck up here, right?"

I can't believe I just managed to string together a few sentences like that. I mean, *we're in a cloud*, this situation should be reaping eternal havoc in my normally sane mind.

I feel calm though. Maybe it's because I think I'm still dreaming. Maybe it's the fact that I'm stuck in the sky with a guy who seems really nice. I guess it's the chatting with Dillon that's calmed me and I'm glad I don't have to keep freaking out.

"Hi, I'm Dillon." He sticks out his hand and I shake it.

"Hi, Dillon, I'm Kate." We release hands and sit back on our respective cloud poofs. I could get used to this comfy-cloud-sitting thing, if I was guaranteed a way of getting back down again.

"So, come to the clouds often, Kate?"

There's that sense of humor again. This is one funny guy.

"Nope, I've never been here before actually," I reply. "I never had three heads before today, either, and now look where I am."

"Three heads." Dillon turns and puts one of his hands on each side of my head. "The only head I see is this one, and it's really pretty on its own."

Oh. Whoa. I should totally push his hands away. Shouldn't I? I just met him in unusual circumstances. We're in a cloud. Who knows what he might do? He could crush my cranium for all I know.

Somehow I don't think he's going to do that. His touch is gentle and I'm hypnotized by his gaze.

He removes his hands from my head. "My own head was covered up by a helmet until I landed there." He points down and I know he's talking about the glass city, even though we can't see it right now. "One minute I was at football practice and the next thing I know I'm down there wearing this weird dress. Everyone on the team fell down and started sleeping, even the coach. We all got sucked under glass and then the circle of weird buildings gobbled us up."

"That's kind of what happened to me." I frown in concentration, remembering. "I was at a fundraiser and I accidentally poisoned everyone there with my bad cake. They all died and then we were all down there." I point under the clouds. "I wasn't under the glass ground and this stupid dress appeared on me." I pluck at the red fabric. "I don't normally wear ancient looking robe things."

"I think it's gorgeous on you, but I'm sure you look gorgeous in normal clothes too."

Dillon gets to his feet after he says this, which is too bad as I don't mind all this flattery one little bit.

"Sorry," he apologizes. "I just... this whole situation is crazy..." He runs a hand through his hair as though frustrated.

I stand up. "Now you realize this? I could have flipped out a long time ago. You calmed me down. So thanks."

He smiles again. I grin back at him. The clouds at our feet start to thin out again. They billow and swirl around us. I take in a deep breath of air and the scent that overwhelms me is like the smell at night, just after it rains.

There's ozone in this air. Something electric is passing between the space between us. A space that's steadily growing smaller.

Dillon presses his forehead gently to mine and I don't move. I don't push him away, which is probably what I should do as he's a stranger.

I don't push him away. I wait. I let the cool clouds rush over me. I let Dillon's nearness warm me. Together we float in circles and the hovering mountain flashes past my peripheral now and then.

I close my eyes. Dillon brings his lips closer to mine. Oh my gosh he's going to kiss me and I'll be damned if I know what to do.

This is it! Get ready, Kate! My heart screams at me inside my mind. My logical brain tells me to pull back. There is no way I'm going with logic right now though.

I don't have to, either, because Dillon yanks himself away.

I open my eyes, not knowing when I'd closed them in the first place.

"Where are you going?" I shout after Dillon as he walks away across the sky. He kicks a cloud and plumes of mist go flying.

He yells back at me. "I'm sorry, Kate, I never should have tried that, I—"

Whatever he was about to say gets cut off by a tremendous sucking sensation. A bottomless tingling erupts in my gut. The clouds are no longer solid. Air starts rushing past me as I start to fall. My stomach feels like it's still in the clouds, which isn't true at all. I'm falling fast and in a second or two I'm about to go splat.

Boing!

I hit the ground and my whole body springs back up. I land safely on my feet and my hair falls in front of my face. I can see through my bouncy, dark curls and it would appear all the fancy gold clasps that were holding it in place have fallen out by the sheer force of my springy impact upon the glassy ground.

"Kate!" Dillon calls my name. "Are you all right?"

"I'm fine!" I fling my head up and my curls whip back. "I fell!" I shout. "*We* fell! We bounced!"

"I know, right?" Dillon is wringing his hands nervously. "That was some crazy shit!"

"Hell yeah it was!"

"Where have you been?" A male voice booms.

Oh no. My extra heads are back. Or were they ever gone? Hera's head starts talking too. "What did you see inside that city?" It says.

"Who's talking?" This question is from Dillon.

"You can hear them?" I ask him.

"He can hear us?" Hera says.

"I can hear other voices, Kate." Dillon steps closer to me. "But I don't see your mouth moving."

I nod my original head. "Yeah, those are my two extra heads I told you about."

"I thought you were joking."

"I thought you might have thought that."

"So, young mortal," Zeus' head speaks loudly again. At this rate I might go deaf in my right ear. "You can hear us, but not see us, correct?"

Dillon scratches the back of his neck. He looks very uncomfortable. "Mortal?" He replies. "Yeah, I can hear you, but I don't see any heads other than Kate's beautiful one."

I think Hera's head just gasped at Dillon's comment on the appearance of mine. "Yes, he obviously can't see me." She hisses.

Hello, *jealousy*.

"Where is our son?" Zeus bellows.

"So you have two extra invisible heads." Dillon mumbles.

"You mean Jason?" I ask, still fizzle-brained after boinging off the ground.

"Of course he means Jason." The Hera Head snaps. "Have you forgotten about my son so easily, Kate?"

"What? Oh no." I stumble over my words. I stop looking at Dillon and zone in on reality. If you can call the strange place we're in realistic. "I don't know where Jason is. We were up there." I crane my neck back and so does Dillon. "We saw a floating mountain and–"

"You saw Mount Olympus?" Zeus Head interrupts.

"Kate," Hera Head says. "You need to find Jason now."

"That blonde kid? He's in there." Dillon points at the glass city.

He still looks mighty confused about the voices emanating out the sides of my head. At least his response was coherent.

"So is my friend Shana!" I hurry toward the glass city.

"Hold up!" Dillon shouts and runs after me. "Are you sure you want to go back in there?"

"What is in there?" Hera Head whispers.

"Persephone and Hades." As soon as I say this my body solidifies. I'm halted in my tracks and I can't move.

"Zeus!" Hera Head shouts. "Release her at once or you will drain your powers."

Dillon almost collides into the back of me. He stops and comes around to face me. I'm posed like a runner who is paused in mid-run. One fist in front of me and one behind. My legs are also one in front of the other.

I must look like such a douche.

I gasp. Finally, I can move again. I plonk my arms down at my sides.

"What happened?" Dillon looks concerned. He puts his arm around my shoulders.

"Would you please tell your boyfriend to remove his hand from the inside of my face." Hera Head demands.

"He's not my…" I start to say.

"She's not my…" Dillon jumps away from me.

"What did you mean Zeus would drain all his powers?" I'm questioning my extra-woman-head. It's a tactical maneuver I just invented as a plan to change the subject.

Although, I don't know if I should be offended at the speed in which Dillon removed his arm from my personage when it was suggested he might be my BF.

"We have limited powers here in the Underworld, Kate." Every time Hera Head says my name I feel strange. She talks as though she knows me. "Our kingdom is Mount Olympus, not here."

"We must use the last of our powers to release Jason from that glass city." When Zeus Head commands, my arms start rising, controlled like a puppet.

"What will we do once Jason is here, mighty Zeus? We'll have no way of getting to Mount Olympus." Hera Head disagrees with Zeus Head, so my left arm falls down.

I look at Dillon. I'd shrug my shoulders to confirm that I have no idea what's going on, but I'm not exactly in control of any part of my body from the waist up right now.

"There is a way," Zeus head says. "And Kate will be the one to take us there."

I what?

I'm guessing Hera Head needs no further convincing, because my left arm has risen into the air once again.

"Are you okay?" Dillon asks me, my normal head.

I smile at him at the same time my arms arc outward. The grin is wiped off my face as my palms *smack* together. A loud *bang* and a blitz of golden light explodes out of my hands.

"Ouch!" I yell and start shaking out my hands. Dillon comes forward and takes my palms into his own.

When the brightness fades I look up to see Jason standing there. He looks from me to Dillon who has hold of my hands.

There's a scowl on Jason's face that could wither a rose, if one was growing nearby at the moment.

I yank my hands out of Dillon's. I don't know why I'm feeling self-conscious about Jason seeing our interaction. As far as I know

Jason never even knew I existed until today.

I, on the other hand, have known about *his* existence for two whole years now. Maybe that's why I'm weary of what he thinks might be going on between me and Dillon.

In which case, I feel so fickle sometimes.

"How did you two get here, outside that glass city?" Jason says gruffly. "The last thing I remember was Hades siccing his mortals on us."

"It's a long story," Dillon replies.

"I wasn't asking you," Jason retorts.

Dillon's eyebrows fly upward on his forehead in response to Jason's snappish comment.

I clear my throat in attempts at defusing the awkward situation. "Something happened up there." I point at the dull gray sky above. "We saw Mount Olympus."

"You saw Mount Olympus?" Jason interrupts, but I continue to gaze upward.

I can't see the clouds Dillon and I had sat on up there. We did fall though, so I know there must be clouds somewhere in that sky. "We fell down here and then your parents clapped my hands for me and you appeared right there." I start walking forward. "Now, Zeus, Hera," I say, talking directly to my other heads like I've never done before. "Do that same clap thing and get my best friend Shana out of there."

"We can't do that, Kate."

My feet lock in place. I can't take another step. Dillon and Jason catch up to me.

"What are you doing?" Dillon asks me. I'm waving my arms around like crazy, trying to get my feet to move.

They won't budge.

"Stop fighting, Kate," Zeus Head implores. "We won't have the power to rescue your friend if you don't cooperate."

I deflate. My shoulders slump and they feel extra heavy. I guess I'm going to have to do whatever they say if I want to get my best friend out of there. I want to get out of here too. Out of this crazy reality, because if I'm not dreaming then we're all in big trouble.

"What do we do now?" Jason asks.

"Now, we go to Mount Olympus," Zeus Head replies.

"How exactly do we get to the great Mount Olympus?" I throw my hands up in the air, just to check and make sure I've got control of my upper limbs.

"You and your boyfriend Dillon are going to take us there," Zeus Head replies.

Dillon goes red in the face. I look at Jason who scowls ever deeper.

"I said he's not my...wait... *we* are going to take us there?"

"I understand what you are thinking, Zeus," Hera Head says. "Kate," she intones into my left ear. "You said you saw Mount Olympus and the Underworld from the sky, correct?"

I nod my middle head and Dillon nods his only head in answer to Hera Head's question.

"She was in the place of the lost?" Jason mumbles. "But that's just a myth. No god or mortal has ever returned from the sky place."

A myth? Is he saying the clouds Dillon and I sat on are a myth within the myth of the Greek gods? Wow. Talk about confusing. I just barely came to accept being in the Underworld as reality and not a dream, what fantasy stories am I going to hear about next?

"So no one has actually seen this sky place before?" Dillon

scratches his chin. In the distance there's a feint rumbling noise. No one but me seems to have heard it though, so I don't say anything. "How did Kate and I get there then?"

"We will not be able to find that out until we get to Mount Olympus." Zeus Head sounds impatient. "The sky place was a myth about lost souls who never reached the Underworld."

"Do you mean Dillon and I discovered the sky place?" I clap my hands, feeling strangely thrilled at this thought. "Cool, I guess that means we get to name it." I too start scratching my chin, feeling thoughtful.

"We don't have time for—"

I interrupt Zeus Head. "I know!" I shout. "We'll call it Limboland."

Jason gawks at me. "Limboland?"

"Yeah, you know." I smile at him. "Limbo is supposed to be that place for souls between Heaven and Hell, right?"

"Enough of this mortal existential philosophizing!" Hera Head starts yelling. "Zeus, how are Kate and her boyfriend—"

"He's not my—"

Hera head keeps talking, interrupting my interruption. "How are they going to get us to Mount Olympus?"

"I don't know how we're supposed to get us to this Mount Olympus place." Dillon points a finger to his left. "Wherever it is we're going though, we should probably leave now.

Everyone looks up.

In the distance an army approaches, led by a flying Persephone and a walking Hades who must be controlling the forward motion of his mortal troops with his body.

I gasp in surprise. That must have been the rumbling noise I'd heard. It was the door of that glass city opening.

"Hurry!" Zeus Head commands. "Dillon, Kate, do whatever it was you did to get to the sky place."

"Limboland!" I shout in a panic. I don't know why it's important that I get to name the place, especially at a time like this. *Concentrate, Kate!* I mentally steel myself. *You don't want to get taken into that city again, especially if it means doing so will make it so you can't save Shana!*

"Kate!" Jason yells. "Seriously?"

The noise of the approaching army is rising.

"The only thing I remember is that I touched Kate's arm and then we were in the... Limboland," Dillon says, instead of "sky place".

"You two were holding hands just now." Jason growls and I think he seems to be aiming some anger at me with his eyes.

"Both of you take one of Kate's hands," Zeus Head commands.

Jason grabs my right hand and Dillon my left.

When nothing happens my panic deepens. The approaching army is only a few hundred yards away now. Their stomping motions making the glass ground tremble beneath my feet.

"Take us to... Limboland, you two!" Zeus Head demands.

"I don't know how!" Dillon and I shout at the same time.

"What were you thinking when you went there before?" Zeus Head sounds more impatient with every passing second. I can't blame him. We're about to be seized!

"I was freaking out when Dillon grabbed my arm inside the glass city!" I yell. "The people were about to jump us!"

"Well they are about to jump you again, so think about that, all three of you!" Hera Head is the one to screech this time.

I do think about being jumped. I think about being captured by the oncoming crowd. It's a reality that's staring me in the face. The army is only a few paces away now when a golden mist builds around my ankles. It swirls upward, drowning out exterior noises.

I can't see anything, only gold smoke. Then, all of a sudden, the whole Underworld is gone entirely from sight.

*

We've arrived.

We're standing in the clouds.

The cloudlike golden mist fades from my vision, swirls down to feet level, and disappears.

I'm still holding hands with Jason and Dillon. I'm sure they're both hating it, because they are also holding hands with each other. We're in a small circle of three. Not counting my two extra heads, because they haven't said anything yet.

"So the sky place is real." Jason cranes his neck around, checking out this lofty environment.

"Yeah, Limboland is real. As real as that floating island over there."

As soon as I say this both Jason and Dillon snap their heads around.

"Mount Olympus," Jason mumbles. "I've never seen it from this perspective. I don't think anyone has but you two."

"You mean us five," I correct him. "We're all up here now."

"Five?" Dillon says. "It's just us three."

"I'm talking about my extra heads." I wink at him like I'm suddenly some kind of extra-heads-expert.

"They're not on your shoulders, Kate."

I look at Jason. He's frowning at me. He seems to be doing that a lot recently.

"That's weird," I say. "I didn't hear your parents say anything when I was up here with Dillon, either." Which is a good thing. I don't tell either of them that I'm secretly glad my other heads are gone. If it takes being up in some sky place for me to have just one head, I'm very okay with that.

A breeze kicks up. I don't know what sky we're floating in. There's air movement and it's exactly like the skies of home. My Earthly home. I can't believe it's gotten to the point where I have to think of the name of the planet I live on.

Earth definitely isn't the only world that's part of my life anymore.

The windy air pushes us. Clouds swirl and we're collectively brushed sideways.

"Oh my Father!" Jason yells. As we float away, I presume he means "oh my God", because his dad is one.

I am, however, super duper amused, and I laugh out loud.

"I didn't notice the ground down there before." Jason looks down. "It's... it's... we're above the—"

"Above the Underworld, yes!" My vocal volume increases, because the wind is really starting to blast now.

"Kate, I don't know why my parents' heads are gone from your shoulders. They weren't visible inside that glass city either!"

"So what are we supposed to do now?" Dillon shouts in response.

"We're supposed to get to Mount Olympus!" I yell.

"I don't think that's going to happen!" Dillon replies. "Look."

Jason and I follow his gaze. We're being blown in the opposite direction of the floating island.

"Oh no!" Jason bellows. "We have to get to the kingdom of the gods!" He pulls his hand out of Dillon's, which turns out to be a really bad move.

If I thought it was windy before it's nothing compared to the gale force winds that blast me in two directions at once.

Jason's grip is being tugged by my right hand by an unseen force. Dillon is equally being pulled away from my left hand. It's going to be impossible to keep a grip on both of them and Dillon is about to lose out first. Not only is his hand being pulled from mine, it's also going in a downward direction. It's as though I'm struggling to lift a teenage guy who weighs over two-hundred pounds.

My right arm is stretched by Jason who is being pulled sideways. His entire body is gravitating toward the floating island.

"Don't drop me, Kate." Dillon doesn't shout these words. His eyes look pleadingly at me as my fingers fail him. His hand is wrenched from my own by force.

I don't even see him fall, because the whip-like effect of Dillon's departure has a rubberband result on me and Jason.

We're both flung through the air. We hold fast to each other as we sail through clouds. Our destination is clear. We're about to crash into the giant floating mountain and somehow I don't think we'll be saved this time by any kind of bounce.

I was right. Even though I really, really didn't want to be.

The closer we fly toward Mount Olympus, the bigger it looks. Soon we're soaring over hills and the landscape no longer looks like a floating island. We're in a land where, even at this great height, I can see all the colors of the ground below are extra vibrant. Reds, blues and greens flash by my vision like light. There are so many more colors rushing by below, my eyes can't take it all in.

Jason manages to draw me toward him as we streak though the

air. He wraps his arms around my waist and I cling to his shoulders.

Our flight slows. Below, a grand city comes into view. All the buildings are made of stone and each one is stabilized by grand columns. The city flows up the side of Mount Olympus.

A dream comes back to me. A dream I'd dreamt last night. A powerful place. *This* powerful place that we're hovering above right now.

At the top of the hill is the grandest structure of all. The stone columns at its entrance are so huge that people who are standing at the bottom look like tiny ants.

We slow down even more and finally my feet are under me, instead of flying out behind. We're practically floating now. I've still got my arms wrapped tightly around Jason's shoulders and as we descend he tightens his hold around my waist.

When we touch down it's not onto the ground. We've landed on the domed top of the highest building. It's windy up here, but it's certainly not as blasting as flying through the air.

I risk a glance down. The hem of my dress is shredded from buffering wind effects.

I also notice something else about the bottom of my dress.

It's glowing with sparking golden mist.

"What's happening now?" I shriek over the noisy wind.

Jason follows my gaze downward. The dome roof we're standing on is massive and transparent. We're perched on top of a crystal clear roof that's so see-through and sparkling I swear it's made out of cut crystal or something.

Jason hasn't answered my question, and he doesn't need to. The swirling gold smoke at my feet billows outward. It's coming from underneath the dome. Soon, the glittering mist penetrates the transparent roof. Great plumes of ethereal smoke build to a height that's just above my head before dissipating.

What's left in its place are two vaguely familiar faces.

Or should I say, familiar heads?

When one of the people now standing in front of Jason and I, starts to speak, my suspicions are confirmed.

"We're free of your shoulders at last, Kate," Zeus Head says. Except, he's not just a head any longer. He's a whole being who is standing next to the entire embodiment of Hera.

They're both wearing white robes. Hera's dress is long while Zeus' is short, like Jason's.

"Come with us, girl," Hera says, not addressing me by name. "There is much to prepare for."

"Son." Zeus nods at Jason. "We know what Hades is planning and it's time to prepare."

"Prepare for what?" Jason still hasn't let me go, and because we're on top of a windy roof, I'm not about to remove my arms from around his neck any time soon either.

"You saw all those mortals Hades and Persephone have gathered in the Underworld." Hera raises her voice when a particularly nasty gust of wind blasts by. "They've built an army and will be invading Mount Olympus soon."

An army?

I lower my arms so they're flat upon Jason's chest. I look up at him. "My friend Shana is back there in that crazy Underworld place!" I shout. "And Dillon..." My voice trails off for a moment. "He fell from the sky in Limboland!"

Without thinking about the potential slipperiness of the surface I'm standing on, I take a step forward. "We have to get back there, we have to get Shana out of there!"

"No, Kate, wait!" Jason screams, but it's too late. I've already gone one step too far. My foot goes out from under me and before I realize I'm falling I'm already flat on my butt. I slip and slide down the curved glass roof. When I hit the edge I grab on with all my might as my legs fling out to the side and around in a great arc.

I'm hanging on by my fingertips, dangling off the side of one very high building.

"Help!" I screech. My feet seem to paddle through the air of their own accord, trying to find purchase on something solid. My skirts flap and billow all around me.

"You shouldn't be so hasty, you know, Kate. It can lead you into terrible situations." Zeus is speaking normally to me as though there's nothing amiss with my precarious hold on the edge of the roof.

Well, there's no need for him to be alarmed. He's floating in the air beside me. The lower half of his body is encased in swirling golden mist and I can't help noticing his arms are still crossed.

"Let's get you down from there now."

Zeus unfolds his arms and reaches a hand toward me. There's someone else reaching toward me too. Jason's head has just appeared, peering over the edge of the roof. He grabs my arm at the same time Zeus touches my shoulder and the entire crystal ceiling explodes.

When glass bursts, it really shatters everywhere.

Once again I find myself being hurtled through the air. This time though, there are sharp pieces of glass being flung along the wind beside me.

I tumble through a blue sky. Falling toward my doom. Shards of glass are my only company on this whirling, tumbling journey toward certain death.

The sound of tinkling, falling glass is the first to hit a hard surface.

The sound of *boing* is the next noise that penetrates my hearing like a sprung spring.

I've hit the ground and bounced. The only other time that's ever happened was when I'd hit the glass surface of the Underworld after falling from the skies of Limboland.

When I land safely on my feet, it's confirmed.

I'm back in the Underworld and Jason is right here with me.

"You bounced too?" I say to his shocked looking face.

He nods at me, wide eyed, then he surveys his surroundings. "We're back," Jason states. "We're in the glass city."

I nod my head as well. We're in the clearing we got busted in. The place where that Persephone woman saw me when I'd failed to duck in time to Hades weird body movements.

We're alone here now. Jason and I.

"Where is everyone? Where is Shana?"

"How did we get here?" Jason doesn't answer my questions, he's got too many of his own. "Kate," he says and grabs my shoulders. "Were you thinking of this place when my father and I tried to stop you from falling?"

I nod, yet again. "Of course I was. I can't just let my friend get turned into some kind of zombie soldier, now can I?"

"So you do know what's going on."

"Well it's not hard to figure out." I step back a little and my sandaled foot crunches broken glass.

I look down. We both look down. Jason releases my shoulders and we step wider apart from each other.

The shards of glass that had fallen with us are glowing a golden hue. Each piece brightens briefly before finally snuffing out. The shards of glass from Mount Olympus merge into the floor beneath our feet, turning opaque and no longer crystal clear.

"This place sucks the life out of everything," I say, looking up once again into Jason's eyes. Jason's blue, blue eyes.

How I'd hate to see the color of his irises fade in this awful place. That's exactly what I remember seeing now. When I'd watched the eyes of the transfixed people in this very place, I'd noticed their irises were the same dull gray in color. Lifeless eyes. Staring eyes.

"Your parents said Hades was building an army." Jason doesn't respond, he just listens to me. "I think they were right." I try kicking at one of the now gray shards of crystal. It won't budge. It's stuck fast into the foggy glass floor.

"This city moved." I splay my arms wide, then let them drop. "It moved on top of all those people who died after eating my cake." I start pacing the floor, ticking off reasons on my fingers. "The people were under the glass ground out there. I dug Shana out of the ground. The city moved on top of those people. They came up inside here, then Hades controlled them and did all those fight moves."

Bang, bang, bang.

There are suddenly thunking noises from overhead. I stop pacing and look up.

"There's someone up there!" I shout and point. Jason cranes his neck back and looks up too. He looks back down and darts away.

"Where are you going?" I shout and run after him. He enters a gaping hole in one of the glass buildings, which I assume is an entrance-way.

When I reach the threshold I hesitate for only a moment. It's dark inside, although I can see a winding staircase made of natural occurring foggy glass. That's what all these buildings look like. The glass isn't smooth, it's slightly lumpy as though someone molded each structure out of opaque gray glass that was once the texture of clay before it hardened. There are no sharp edges anywhere.

I climb the steps and come out onto a landing. There before me is Jason. He's standing in front of a wall of glass boxes. The glass of the wall is a little more see-through, like some of the outer windows in each of the glass buildings that make up this strange city.

The large glass boxes contain people. One person in each box. Young looking people. Teenagers, to be precise. I'm looking at a row of trapped teens who look to be about the same age as Jason and I. Also similar to us, every single teenager behind that glass wall is wearing ancient Greek garb. The guys are dressed in gladiator looking apparel while the girls seem to all be wearing white toga like dresses.

"Help!" They cry.

"Get them out of there, Kate." Jason says this to me as if I'm holding a glass key or something.

He turns and comes toward me. "Remember how you freed Shana from the glass ground?"

My eyebrows raise up on my forehead. "Oh yeah, I totally busted that glass wide open, didn't I?"

Without another thought on the matter I hurry forward and make a fist. I draw back my hand then I punch the glass wall.

Nothing happens. I hit at it again and again. Nothing gives.

Snap.

Pop.

A crack appears in the wall. Then another. It spreads like a spider's web. I back slowly away as the crack runs outward across the entire expanse of glass wall.

Boom!

The glass boxes shatter and fall into a million pieces.

"Wow," someone says.

"That was epic," a girl intones.

"Thanks," another guy comments.

After stepping their way over glass chunks as huge as bricks, the now freed teenagers meet me and Jason on shard-free ground.

Everyone starts talking at once.

"Quiet, please!" Jason barks.

Everyone shuts up.

"One at a time, each of you." He points at a girl. "How did you get here?"

"I was at my friends' birthday party and everyone passed out." Her eyes are wide and she moves her hands around expressively. "When I woke up we were all underneath the ground that I could see through. Then these buildings rolled over me and I got sucked out of the ground wearing this." She stop talking and twirls around. "It's a nice dress, I could wear it to the prom or something."

I'm not really sure why this girl suddenly cares about what she's going to wear to a high school dance, so I clear my throat, urging her to continue.

She looks at me. "This crazy lady wearing a black dress scooped me off the ground and threw me in here."

When the girl is finished talking everyone else tells their stories quickly. They're all similar tales. They'd been at large social gatherings before passing out and ending up here.

"How come your dress is red?" A shy girl asks quietly.

"It's because she's a demigod of Olympus while you are all halflings of the Underworld."

What the heck did Jason just say?

"It's true, Kate." He looks at me now. "It's the reason my parents attached themselves to you. It's the reason I was placed at your high school two years ago."

Now I'm really confused. Is he saying he knows what's been going on this whole time and he never said a word about it until now?

"So it's your fault my friend Shana is missing somewhere in this stupid Underworld place?"

I think the other teenagers sense tension between us, because they back away and start talking amongst themselves.

"No," Jason shakes his head. "I didn't know what my parents were doing when I saw their heads on your shoulders at the grocery store."

I gasp, remembering when Shana and I had bumped into him as we'd picked out ingredients for our stupid cake. "So that's why you looked at me so funny!"

He nods. "I only knew it was Hades when I touched Shana's head and that glass floor spread out over everyone at the fundraiser. I knew my parents meant we needed to follow those people here. It was how they found out that Hades is planning an attack on Mount Olympus."

"Why is he using people?"

"Mortals."

"Whatever." I wave my hand, dismissively. "We're just people you know."

"Because mortals have never been to the Underworld, Kate. Only their souls enter this realm after they die. Not their physical bodies."

I clap a hand to my mouth at this latest revelation. "So I really didn't kill them with my terrible cake?"

"No, of course you didn't." Jason takes my hand gently away from my mouth. "And I know something else my parents don't seem to understand."

I look up at him, transfixed on his slow words.

"You're not just a halfling, Kate, you're a demigod."

"Yeah, you said that before." I frown. "What the heck is a halfling and what's a demigod?"

"They are halflings." Jason indicates the ancient clad teens. "Children of half-gods of the Underworld. Each person here has one parent who is mortal and one who is a demigod of the Underworld. It's why my parent's attached themselves to you. They suspected this is truly who you were."

"Whoa. Hold on." I rub my temples. Confused. "So we're all one quarter Underworld god?"

"Nope," Jason smiles a little. "They are part Underworld god. You, Kate, are half demigod of Olympus and I know who your goddess mother is."

"Um, excuse me," I snort. "I know who my mother is, and even though she acts like a goddess sometimes, she's just Melanie Nicholls and she's not magical."

The ground begins to tremble. One of the guys wearing a gladiator dress runs to the clear window. "It's them." He presses his hands to the glass. "That crazy lady and that man are back with our friends."

I don't have to look out that window myself to know that the shaking floor is being caused by a marching army. An army that consists of human beings that are being controlled. One of whom is my best friend.

"What are we going to do?" A girl squeals and hugs the person nearest too her.

"Kate," Jason steps closer toward me. "Do your thing."

"My thing?"

He winks at me. It brightens my soul.

"Oh *that* thing." I wink right back at him and get ready to punch the ground.

"Everyone get ready to run." Jason nods at me after everyone else readies themselves nearest the entrance to the stairwell.

I kneel and punch the glass floor with my fist.

And of course nothing happens. I just end up with really sore knuckles, so the next time I try I pound at the surface with the outer right side of my fist.

Suddenly, the whole building goes bump. The entire structure shifts and begins to lean.

"Oh no!" A girl's voice cries out. I look to were she's pointing. Amidst the fallen glass rubble, a smoky mist rises. I can see the outline of a black clad woman appearing.

It's Persephone, and she's about to discover us all.

Jason draws me close. His hands pull me toward him and he whispers into my ear. "Think about Shana, Kate. This is the only way to save your friend."

I do think about Shana. I think about her really hard. I stomp my feet on the floor, which doesn't have any affect.

Persephone's form is solidifying.

Teenagers are screaming and running away down the stairs.

Jason presses into me. He draws his face away from my ear and slides his lips along my cheek. "Think and feel, Kate." He growls.

"Feel the power I know is within you."

His lips cover mine. My whole world warms. Of their own devices my hands tangle up into Jason's hair. He kisses me and I'm like an explorer discovering new land. My very first kiss surveys the lips of this guy who is a god. My inner goddess responds and I know immortal bliss.

A thunderous blast erupts under my feet and our kiss is obliterated into smithereens.

*

I think Persephone got me. All I see is gray and white smoke. When the fog finally clears though, I can see we're all right.

Well, all right as can be considering we're in the deepest depths of the Underworld right now. All around are hundreds of people. Some coughing, others screaming, a few casually chatting. Most importantly, no one is zombified. They're all awake.

Also, there are no glass buildings. Nothing. Not even a shard of glass in sight.

So the buildings hadn't exploded from the dynamite kiss I'd shared with Jason. The glass structures had completely vanished.

"Nooooooo!" A woman's voice screeches from overhead. And up overhead is where Persephone and Hades are hovering. "Everything is destroyed, everything is ruined!" She howls. "You!" Her finger points an almost visible stabby path, from her place in the skies, to my forehead. "This is all your doing."

"You will pay," Hades grumbles. He's floating on a black wind while Persephone hovers next to him on a foggy grayish cloud.

Their respective mists don't stay separate for long though. When Hades and Persephone merge together in the air, so do their smoky clouds.

Now no one is chatting. Everyone is screaming and running. Above us the gods of the Underworld have created a black and white cyclone.

My dress whips up around me as I get to my feet.

"Halflings!" Jason shouts. "All you teenagers hold hands!"

None of us need telling twice. We know who he's talking about. All the young people who were trapped in that building unite. We grasp hands and form a line, just as Dillon comes barreling out of the hysterical crowd.

"What happened? What's going on?" He yells and looks at the point where my hand holds tightly to Jason's.

"Here!" I scream and reach for Dillon. As I do the black and white striped tornado from above slashes down from the sky. "Take my hand!" I bellow at Dillon.

Our fingertips meet. He slides his palm swiftly into my own just as every mortal and demi-god alike gets sucked into a swirling hurricane of smoke and mist.

*

My alarm clock goes off with a dream-shredding blare. I sit up to discover I'm not in bed. The alarm sound is the wailing noise of the school fire-alarm ringing throughout the auditorium.

I'm holding Jason's hand in my right palm, and Dillon's hand is clasped tightly in my left. Dillon's hand that's encased in a glove. I look up and notice he's wearing a whole football uniform in the colors of green and white.

I'm dressed in jeans and a t-shirt and Jason is no longer garbed in his short blue dress.

All around people seem to be waking up.

Everyone is here. All are accounted for. All those who took part in eating my deadly cake are alive and well. And there's more. All the teenagers who had held hands are now here too.

"Kate!" I look up to see Shana stepping her way around people toward me.

"Shana!" I cry and release both Dillon's and Jason's hands. They're both sitting up now, looking flummoxed.

When I reach Shana I throw my arms around her in a huge hug. "Can you believe what happened?" She gushes. "I can't believe it! I can't believe it!"

The fire-alarm shuts off at the same time all the outer doors along the far wall burst open.

Paramedics, fire-fighters and police officers swarm the gym. Shana is guided away from me to an ambulance outside and eventually I too get poked and prodded by a team of medics.

I'm sitting on the edge of the ambulance when Dillon walks up to me. His helmet is gone from his head and so are the huge shoulder pads. He's got a scratchy looking blanket wrapped around his shoulders.

"So," he says, sitting next to me. "That wasn't just a dream."

I shake my head and look up at him. "No, I guess it wasn't."

"Pretty crazy." He smiles, and when he does, it makes me feel giddy and my eyes start to water. A huge grin spreads across my face and I bark out a slightly insane laugh.

"I don't think spending time with you in those clouds was all that bad though, Kate."

I sigh. I can't help it. I know perfectly well Dillon isn't talking about the second time we'd ended up in Limboland. He's talking about when we'd almost kissed.

Almost being the key point. What would have happened to all of us if Dillon hadn't walked away from me when he had, up in the setting of those fluffy white clouds? Would we be here now? Would I have kissed Jason?

Jason. He's walking toward us now. I look from him to Dillon and back again.

"Can I ask you a question, Kate?" Dillon asks me as Jason strides up. "Do you drive?"

I frown. "Yeah, I do, why?"

"Well, I'm not exactly from around here."

"Oh my gosh! You mean?"

"Yep, wherever it is that Underworld place landed me now, it's a couple hundred miles from my home town."

"No problem," I say, standing up from the emergency vehicle. "I'll drive you home. We'll make it a road-trip."

"I'm coming too." Jason speaks for the first time since he arrived. "Here you go, Kate, I got this for you inside the gym. Thought it might help calm your nerves."

"Wow, thanks," I say, taking the triple layer icecream cone out of Jason's hand. "And of course you're coming with us, oh godly one. You've got a lot of otherworldly explaining to do." I smirk at him.

A police officer approaches and takes Dillon's and then Jason's statements. When it comes time for me to start talking I don't even have to move my mouth, because my two extra heads start gabbing away for me.

Apparently they're back upon my shoulders, but I'll be damned if I'm going to let either one of them have a lick of my icecream. I thought for sure I'd left the two heads far behind on the land of Mount Olympus.

I know one thing for sure; that kiss I'd shared with Jason opened something within me and I'm definitely not in any mood to let Zeus and Hera camp out on my shoulders for long. I feel like I know myself better. I feel like there is power within me, and I tap into it now.

I shrug my shoulders. Hera Head and Zeus Head both topple off, appear solid for a moment on the ground, and then vanish.

The police officer jumps back in surprise when he sees the heads, and Dillon rises to his feet to catch him as he faints.

"My parents will return, you know." Jason warns me with a wink. "They're persistent and I'm pretty sure they want to learn more about you, Kate."

I shove one hand into the pocket of my jeans, grateful that I'm no longer wearing a heavy dress. I bite into the top head of icecream on my cone.

"I know your parent's will be back," I say. I bite a cold chunk out of the second scoop of icecream, saving the chocolate layer for last. "I'll be ready and waiting for them with shoulder-pads made of spikes."

I wink right back at him.

STORY II

Dating A God

What is it with parents? They're so overprotective sometimes. Okay, so maybe my mom *is* slightly justified in her paranoia. I mean, just a few months ago I *did* almost get sucked into the Underworld for all eternity.

It wasn't like it was my fault this almost happened. It was Hades' and Persephone's doing. I guess sometimes the gods get power-hungry, which is exactly what happened at the beginning of my senior year. The lord of the Underworld and his powerful companion got it into their godly heads that they would control an army of human soldiers and storm Mount Olympus in attempts at taking it over. Why anyone would want to rule over any large body of land, is beyond me. I'm having enough trouble as it is trying to get all my studies done *and* hold down a social life.

Talking of which, my dating life would be non-existent if Mom had her way. She doesn't exactly like my boy of choice.

See, the thing is, I'm trying to date a god.

Mom knows what he is. Everyone in this town knows about the Underworld incident a few months ago. Things like that don't go unnoticed when fifteen percent of the population get sucked into the Underworld, and then spewed back out again.

To be honest, I'm surprised at how well the community is taking this new information. It's as though discovering the existence of ancient gods is just a bit of gossip. I would have thought coming to terms with such a revelation would take some getting used to.

Not so for the residents of Lakepoint. We keep ourselves to ourselves and our town business within our own district. I guess there's really no point in blabbing about supernatural deities to national governments anyway, they'd think our water was poisoned or something, and that we'd all gone insane.

"Kate," Mom points a finger at me. "Don't you realize how dangerous dating this boy could be?"

"He's not exactly a boy, Mom." Flicking my long dark hair over my shoulder, I scoop up my book bag.

"Exactly my point! He's eighteen years old, same as you, and he's a... he's a..."

I don't think Mom can bring herself to say it, so I fill in the blank for her. "He's a god."

Her face crinkles indignantly and then she shakes her head. "I don't think I'll ever get used to hearing that term being bantered around town."

"Well, you might want to try." Opening the front door of our house, I'm about to head outside.

"Don't you dare walk out on this conversation, young lady."

Huffing out a great big sigh, I turn to her. "I'm going to be late for school."

"Oh." Mom frowns. "Well, we'll pick up this discussion when you get home, so don't think that you can just go accepting any dating offers from that... that..."

I'm about to say *god* again, but Mom turns away mumbling angrily to herself.

Shrugging my shoulders, I close the door behind me. She's the one who just dared to walk away from our little conversation. And she doesn't know it, but I'm the one who is definitely going to dare to date a god. I just have to get to school a little early today, so that I can tell Jason I'm accepting his offer of a get-together on Saturday.

*

When I arrive at school there's still some gossip in the halls about gods and goddesses. There's one person who's benefited from the knowledge of deities existing, and he just so happens to be walking straight toward me right now.

It's Jason Fulmen. The source of the gossip. Not that he's the one who starts all the gossip mongering. He's the one who everyone is talking about. After all, he *is* a god. Or from what he's told me. He's the son of a god. Apparently Zeus and Hera created him eighteen years ago. So he's a new god, like I'm a new demi-goddess. At least, that's what Jason keeps telling me.

Ever since the Underworld incident a few months ago, Jason is convinced he knows who my goddess mother is. He says she resides on Mount Olympus and that I should really consider meeting her soon. In my opinion though, due to the fact that nothing goddess-like has happened to me since the Underworld mishap, I'm not in any way inclined to believe Jason right now. I know for a fact that my mother is Mrs. Melanie Nicholls, wife to Mr. Richard Nicholls; my dad.

Jason saunters ever closer to me down the hall. When he reaches me he gives me a crooked grin that kind of makes my knees wobble.

He's just so darned good looking! I don't know if it's because he's an Olympian god, or if he uses really expensive shampoo, but for some reason Jason's long ish blonde hair glows with effervescent abandon!

His lips are moving. I think he's saying something. Why oh why do I get so dreamy-headed whenever Jason's around? "Kate?" He waves a hand in front of my face. "Mount Olympus to Kate... did you ask your parents?"

"What?" I say, zoning into reality. "Oh! Yeah, I talked to my mom, but she said..."

My voice trails off. I told myself I was going to do this. I am going to go on a date with a god. Not that I really consider Jason to be some kind of lightning bolt wielding lord of the heavens, or anything like that. I mean, he's the same age as me. Besides, nothing other-worldly or god-like has happened since the Underworld incident. I don't know why Mom is so worried about me dating an ordinary boy.

Well, as ordinary as the son of a god can be with his major good looks and...

"Kate!" Jason snaps his fingers in front of my face, snapping me out of my wandering thoughts.

"Sorry! Yes! My Mom said it was fine, dude." Tucking a strand of hair behind my ear, I pretend like I'm perfectly coherent in Jason's presence, and not at all overwhelmed by his animal magnetism. Or should I say *god-like mesmerism?* "We can totally go on a date."

"Okay!" Jason beams a great big smile. "That's great!" He claps his hands together. "I'll pick you up tonight!"

I can't help but smile right back at him, real large like. "Awesome! See you later! Wait!" I catch myself as he turns to leave. "I'll just meet you at the movies, okay?"

Phew. That was close. Wouldn't want Jason showing up at my house until I can convince Mom that this particular god-boy is perfectly datable.

"Are you sure?"

I nod in reply to Jason's question and that settles it. I'm going on an official date tonight. Everything is going to be terrific, and normal. It's only a date. Just because crazy magical things happened once, many months ago, doesn't mean they'll ever occur again. The only magical thing that's going to happen tonight is that I'm going to get a kiss from Jason.

At least, I hope I will.

*

School was epic. Never thought I'd mentally admit such a thing to myself. Normally every class is agony. Today though, I'd been on a high looking forward to tonight's date.

Back when the Underworld incident happened, I remember what it was like to kiss Jason in another dimension. Funnily enough, I'd almost kissed another guy on a cloud.

Tonight, I want to find out what it's like to kiss someone on the ground.

After checking out my ensemble for the evening in the full length mirror, I head out the door and down the street. I'd told Mom and Dad that I'm sleeping over at Shana's tonight, and my best friend forever is totally going to cover for me if they call her house.

When I get to the movie theater I can see Jason is already there. He's standing with his hands in the pockets of his jeans. Different jeans than the ones he wore at school.

Hooray! He made an effort for our date.

"Hi!" I say exuberantly, bouncing up. "What are we gonna see?"

"It's up to you." Jason smiles at me before looking at the long row of movie posters along the outer wall of the theater.

Hmmmm. I ponder to myself, wondering which one looks best. "I know!" I shout, pointing a finger at my poster of choice. "Let's see

Swarm."

Jason is still smiling. "Are you sure a movie about killer bees won't give you nightmares?"

Nudging him playfully on the arm, we both giggle before heading inside the theater. I order some fruity flavored candies at the snack bar, and Jason gets us a Coke with two straws. Aw, isn't sharing sweet?

When we get inside the actual theater is when the conundrum begins. Where will he chose to sit? If he picks a random pair of seats anywhere but the very back row, I'll know he actually wants to watch the movie. After all, everyone knows the highest, farthest seats in the theater are for making out.

Jason is walking up the lit up steps, drink in hand. He's still moving up. Score! He's sat down all the way at the end of the back row.

Looks like I'll be getting more than just one kiss on the ground tonight. When I say ground, I mean a kiss somewhere normal, instead of under dire circumstances caused by one power-hungry Hades.

The theater dims. The movie starts. Jason lifts the arm between us on the chairs and cuddles closer to me. Leaning left, I cozy myself into his side after he puts his arm around my shoulders. As an excuse to get Jason to hold me tighter, every time there's a super freaky scene during the movie, I make sure to jump in my seat to seem extra scared.

It works. Jason squeezes me tight. "Told you we shouldn't have seen this movie."

I look up at him. He smiles down at me. He moves in close. Slowly. Closer still. His lips are about to touch mine. This is it. The moment I've been waiting for since things abnormally turned my life upside down all those months ago. I'm going to get a kiss. A real and normal kiss from a guy in a perfectly normal theater.

We both remove our 3D glasses that we'd put on before the movie started. His lips touch mine ever so gently. Pushing upwards I attempt to deepen the kiss, but the movie is getting really loud. Seriously, do they have to crank the surround sound to such ear blowing levels? How's a girl in the back row supposed to get in a decent make-out session when it sounds like the bees in the movie are actually swarming around her head?

"Argh!" More than one audience member starts screaming. "Get them off me!" I hear someone shout. "I'm getting stung! Aaarrrggghhh!"

Screaming. Panic.

I look up from our kiss to find that the Dolby stereo noises are no longer only coming from the movie screen.

"Bees!" Jason yells. Everyone in the crowd is on their feet screaming, waving their arms all over the place as a stream of bees swarms right out of the movie screen.

"What's happening?" I jump to my feet trying to shoo bees away from my face. "Is this some kind of twisted prank by the theater staff?"

"Take my hand, Kate, quick!"

Through the chaos of people trying to crowd their way down the center aisle of stairs, I find Jason's hand. The moment I grasp it a sense of safety envelopes me.

No bees are stinging us. There's an invisible space surrounding Jason and I. The bees bounce off the force-field like aura we seem to be exuding.

"This is the work of the gods!" Jason grips my hand tighter. "Hades must be here, Kate. We have to stop this and help these people!"

"I know right!" I'm used to this. I know how to help. Jason showed me the way to tap into whatever powers I possess when Hades had tried to steal people from Earth, all those months ago. "Let's do this!"

Concentrating on the bees, I squeeze my eyes shut.

"Whoa."

When I open them again a split second later, I echo Jason's statement. "Whoa."

The bees are gone. A few people are still trying to jam out of the theater, but most of them have realized they're no longer almost being stung to death.

Jason lets go of my hand. "Well," he says, scratching his head. "That worked." He looks at me. "What did you do?"

Shrugging my shoulders, I glance around. "I just thought about the bees disappearing."

Jason nods his head. "Nice one." He puts his hand in the air and I high five him.

"Ow!" Looking at the palm of my self inflicted slapped hand, I find more than just one bee sting embedded in my flesh. "Those bees were real, dude."

"I know." Looking concerned, Jason ushers me down the stairs and out of the theater. When we get outside there are already ambulances crashed up along the curb and cop cars screeching into the parking lot, blue and red lights flashing, sirens wailing. It looks like a scene of the apocalypse out here.

Jason has one hand around my waist and he's holding my stung palm at the wrist. Yeah, because I'm too weak to hold up my own arm. I don't mind though, might as well let him be helpful if it means I get to stay in physical contact with him.

"Oooooooh." Moans of agony croon out from the injured as we try to find an ambulance. People are stung all over their faces and arms. One woman must be allergic to bee stings because she's lying flat on a stretcher and a team of paramedics are working on resuscitating her. Her face is so swollen she looks like one giant bee sting.

"I can't believe Hades attacked like this." Tears prick the backs of my eyes. "This is all my fault."

Jason stops walking, forcing me to halt. "What are you talking about, Kate?"

"Hades and Persephone knew it was me who crumbled their stupid glass castle in the Underworld. They weren't exactly happy about it. I ruined their plans of creating human soldier drones to take over Mount Olympus." I look up at Jason. "Now they totally want revenge on me, I just know it!"

"Come here." Jason wraps his arms around me and squeezes me tight. "I shouldn't have said anything, Kate, this is my fault."

Huh? What's he talking about?

"I jumped to conclusions back in the theater. It wasn't Hades."

Pulling away, I look up into his eyes. "What do you mean?"

"I mean, it couldn't have been Hades, because my father has dealt with him."

"He has?"

Jason nods. "After the Underworld incident, Zeus knew what Hades was up too. He has re-enforced the barriers between worlds. Hades and Persephone can't even so much as look anywhere beyond the Underworld now, let alone escape its confines."

"They can't?"

Now Jason shakes his head. "Remember how you revealed your limboland to my dear old dad?"

It's my turn to nod in reply, then, Jason adds, "Zeus has made good use of it to protect this realm and Mount Olympus."

"He has?"

Jason smiles. "See, Kate? This is why we should have had a date a long time ago. We haven't had a chance to talk, have we?"

No we certainly haven't. I'm in full agreement of that. We also haven't had time do anything else. Like kissing, for example. And this time, when I finally managed to get out on a date... when I finally get to touch my lips to his?

Bees.

Bees happen.

Why did bees happen if Hades wasn't responsible? I don't know, but I'm determined to find out.

"Ouch." My stung palm starts stinging again and Jason hurries me away to a free ambulance. I guess finding out who's responsible for the movie swarm will have to wait until I can at least find some tweezers and get these stupid stingers out of my sore skin.

*

After the paramedic removes the stingers from my palm, something strange happens. "Check this out," I say, holding my hand up for Jason to see as we make our way out of the theater parking lot. "The bumps are going away. That paramedic must have used some really good balm or something."

Jason grins. "It's your inner goddess, Kate. You heal from mortal wounds."

Not this again. Ever since I helped stop Hades by using whatever powers I seem to hold within me, Jason has been trying to convince me that it's because I have a goddess for a mother.

I don't know why I can do what I can do, but I definitely know who my own mom is. She's the woman who didn't want me out with Jason tonight.

"I better go."

"Already?" Jason frowns. "But we didn't exactly get to have a real date."

"Yeah, bee swarms coming out of movies really kill a mood, don't they?"

My rhetorical question cheers Jason up and he grins. "How about trying again tomorrow?"

"Well, Shana's having a pool party at her house while her parents are away for the weekend."

"Perfect!" now Jason is smiling really big. "I'll see you tomorrow then." He kisses me so quickly on the lips, I'm slightly taken aback. Too bad I can't dive back in for a lingering kiss. I really should get home before I get busted.

Sadly, Jason and I part ways. Heading up the street, I text Shana that I'll be going home instead of coming to her house. I promise her that I'll definitely be there for her pool party tomorrow.

Fifteen minutes later I creep into the house through the back door. Just when I think I'm home free while making my way downstairs to my basement bedroom, Mom accosts me.

"Kate? What are you doing here?"

Quick, brain! Think of something to say!

"I... I got in a fight with Shana," I blurt. "I'm not talking to her ever again!" Mom looks surprised when her eyebrows shoot up on her forehead. She opens her mouth to say something, but I carry on with my lie, interrupting her. "I don't want to talk about it! I'm going to bed!"

And with that I stomp down the stairs, run into my bedroom and slam the door shut behind me. For added effect I howl loudly into my pillow, so it seems like I'm crying.

After a few minutes I'm guessing Mom's going to leave me alone in my fake sorrow, because she doesn't knock on my door or anything.

Quickly, I text Shana to tell her what I've done. She sends me a message back asking when I decided to become such a liar-liar-pants-on-fire-girl.

JUST COVER FOR ME, OKAY?! XX

I text her again and receive a one letter reply from her in response:

K

That's Shana's message. The letter K, which I hope means she really will cover for me. It's only this one time. How was I supposed to know a swarm of bees would blast out of the movie screen? I can't help feeling a little weirded out by the whole incident. Maybe Shana is just pissed off at me for not spending the night at hers' like I said I would. Well, she doesn't know what I'm going through. I've got to figure out why the bee swarm thing happened, and that's exactly what I'm going to do tomorrow when I meet Jason at her pool party.

When I fail to get any more texts from Shana, I plop my phone onto the nightstand and curl up in bed. Stroking a finger over my palm I find there isn't a single puncture wound remaining from any of the bee stings.

Maybe I should be thinking about how it's possible for me to heal so quickly. It might lead me to understanding what happened at the theater tonight. The only time anything otherworldly ever happens in this town, I always seem to be there to witness it first hand.

Jason is always there too though. I wonder why he let me go so easily tonight. Apart from re-assuring me that Hades couldn't have caused the bee swarm, Jason hadn't really talked with me about who actually could have done it.

As I drift off to sleep I'm thinking I might have to discuss certain things with the gorgeous blonde god at Shana's tomorrow, for sure.

*

Knock. Knock. Knock.

"Kate." Mom's muffled voice floats through door of my bedroom. "Shana's on the phone, I really think you should talk to her."

Sitting bolt upright in bed, the lies I told yesterday come barreling into my consciousness. "Um, just a sec, Mom." Scrambling out of bed I throw on a thin robe, then whip open the door. Feigning peevishness, I let out a loud sigh. "I guess you're right." Grabbing the phone from Mom's outstretched hand I pretend to grudgingly accept Shana's phone call.

"What do you want?" I growl into the home phone handset.

"Be nice to her, Kate," Mom says, striding away. "She's your best friend."

Slamming the door shut for added effect, I shout into the phone until I hear Mom pound her way up the stairs.

"Thanks a lot!" Shana's voice rings out through the phone.

"I'm just joking, chill!" I reply. "I'll tell my mom that we totally made up right after this call, okay?"

"You better."

After confirming with Shana that Jason and I will be at her pool party, I hang up the phone and exit my bedroom. I shower and put on my bikini under my clothes, then I run upstairs with the handset and shove it onto the base in Mom's office to charge.

"I'm going to Shana's!" I shout into the hallway as I don't see either of my parents anywhere. "You were right, Mom. She's my best friend forever!"

"Told you!" Mom's voice echoes from somewhere in the house, I think she's upstairs or something. Just as I'm about to leave her office though, I notice a strange light emanating from the bottom of the closed door on the opposite side of the room.

My mother is a seamstress. Not only is sewing her hobby, but she runs her own business from home. The office I'm standing in is like a small fabric shop. Reams of material line the shelves on one entire wall of this room. In the middle of the room is a space with a raised platform that her customers stand on when she does measurements. Mom has all kinds of sewing machines in here. She even has a big old fashioned loom in one corner that she brought back from a trip to England once. She says she got it at an auction house, but the thing is so old I swear she must have stolen it from a museum. She even uses it sometimes. For what reason, I have no idea. She gets most of her yarn for knitting online.

Inching toward the door at the far end of the room, I'm drawn to the strange rippling blue light that seems to be leaking along the floor.

"Tell Shana I said hi!" Mom yells again from upstairs. I continue towards the glowing door without answering her. "Or maybe I should go with you, Kate. I need to speak with Shana's mom about some dress alterations!"

That's snapped me to attention. I definitely don't want Mom

going with me to Shana's for multiple reasons:

1) She'll find out that Shana's parents aren't even there.

2) Mom will see that there's a pool party going on.

3) Jason will be there. The god she doesn't want me to date.

Turning around quickly, I yell up the stairs as I exit Mom's office. "You can't come with me! I'm leaving now, sorry!" And with that I bang the front door of the house shut behind me and run down the street.

I make it to Shana's in record time and throw myself dramatically onto a deck chair in the back yard. "Phew! I almost got us both busted!"

"You did?" Shana hands me a red slushy drink and I sip it down fast.

"Ow!" I scream, grabbing my head. "Brain freeze!"

"Slow down, dummy!" Shana takes the drink back and puts it down onto a patio table. "Now how did you almost get us busted?"

Calming my breathing helps to relieve the pain of sucking down liquid ice too fast. "My Mom almost came with me just now so she could check *your* Mom's dress measurements!"

Shana shakes her head in disgust. "Told you not to lie so much. Your fibbing is going to get everyone in trouble!"

"Whatever." With a wave of my hand I dismiss the subject of my recent tall tales. "Is Jason here yet?"

Turning half way, Shana points across the pool. "Yeah, he's over there at the edge talking to Amelia who's in the pool."

For the second time today, I sit up straight and alert. "What's he talking to her for?" I don't wait for Shana to answer before I'm jetting my way around the pool. Amelia is the head cheerleader at Lakepoint High. She's been trying to hook up with Jason ever since she found out he's a god.

I mean, if he does want to hook up with Amelia, then what do I care? As far as I'm concerned it's his loss if he loses me because he's so in to checking out her bulging cleavage.

And I really do mean that. As I round the pool I can see that Amelia might have a wardrobe malfunction soon. On purpose. She's totally popping out of her bikini top. I'm sure she wouldn't care if one of her boobs "accidentally" fell out of her barely-there swim suit while Jason gawks at her chest.

He's really staring hard at her ample cleavage and by the time I reach him my face is burning with jealousy.

"Hi." I say coldly.

He doesn't look up, he just remains on bended knee, gaping at Amelia's chest.

"Oh hiiiiii, Kate." Amelia smirks at me, pushing her shoulders back.

"Kate?"

Finally, Jason looks up at me. "What do you think of those?"

"I... I..." I can't believe he just asked me what I think about that slut's boobs! I'm about to pop! My head is going to explode. And then I look where Jason is pointing. He's not indicating Amelia's chestal area at all. He's pointing at the pool water she's standing in.

There are two dark blobs in the water beside her.

"What are you guys doing?" Amelia continues to flaunt her nearly nude body at Jason, who's completely unaware of her advances.

"Um, Amelia?" I'm doubtful about the darkness that's surrounding the voluptuous red headed girl in the pool. "I think you better get out of the water." Actually, I'm starting to panic for everyone in the pool. "Everybody get out of the water right now!"

A few heads turn to look at me. Except for Amelia, she's got her eyes locked on Jason. He, however, has his eyes locked on me. Quickly, he stands up. "Do as she says, everyone!" He screams. "Get out of the wa—"

Jason doesn't get his final word out before a giant *splash* engulfs the occupants of Shana's pool.

Again, just like yesterday at the movies, screaming ensues. Only this time the yelling is punctuated by gurgling sounds, what with all the water spraying everywhere.

"Help me!" Amelia screams as the darkness below her widens across the deepest depths of the pool. Despite the churning waves that lap up over the cement edge, Jason dives into the water.

"Jason!" I cry.

"Kate!" Shana is slipping and sliding her way over to me from around the opposite side of the pool. "What's happening?"

"I don't know!" I shout back at her. "We have to get everyone out of there!" Following Jason's jump into the pool, despite a great inner sense of panic at drowning, I dive in.

And of course I come up spluttering. My feet touch the bottom of the pool, but not when wave after wave continues to pummel me and everyone else in the water who's trying to scramble out.

Splishing and splashing my way towards the nearest person I can see, I manage to coax a girl toward the pool steps. My arms are getting tired by the time I make contact with the next person I'm aiming to assist.

"Kate!" It's Jason. "You need to do your special thing again." He splutters and wipes at his face as another wave attempts to splash its way between us. "We need to defeat this dark entity!"

What dark entity? Looking down through the tumultuous water,

I notice the entire floor of the pool is now completely darkened like a gaping hole into the night sky.

"Oh!" I scream. "*That* darkness!"

I shouldn't have bothered to open my mouth and speak just then, because a huge wave pounds right over my head at that precise moment. I'm taken under the water. Waves crash on and off my face. I can't get a breath in! I'm going to drown!

Ggguuuurrrrggglleeee! Splutter! Pffft, spit, "Aaarrrggghhhh!" I scream when Jason finally manages to heave me out of the depths. He has a tight grip on me with one arm while his other hand grips my own.

"Now, Kate! Concentrate!"

I don't know how I do it, but I manage to think about the darkness below us being gone. Concentrating on forcing the waves to die down stirs my inner goddess. I can feel my power rising. It pushes the excess water from my lungs. I feel like I can breathe properly now. Closing my eyes I'm able to concentrate even harder. I'm aware of a warmth coming from my hand. It's the contact I'm making with Jason. A connection of power zips through us, but there's something else there. Something that feels right, even in this moment of chaos.

Whoosh.

Suddenly, there is no more watery noise.

There is only calm.

I open my eyes to find the calm I'd pictured in my mind has become a reality. The pool waters are steady, only slightly lapping at the edges. Almost half the pool water is gone though, having been blasted out of the cement confines up onto the patio.

Jason and I are left standing together only waist high in water near what should be the deep end of the swimming pool. Glancing around through chlorine soaked eyes, all I can see are drenched teenagers lying around the edge of the pool, coughing and spluttering for dear life.

"You did it." Jason chokes and I'm wondering about his mortality. Can a god of Olympus drown? Somehow I doubt it.

"We did it." I correct him. "Did you feel that..." Swiping yet more wetness from my eyes, my words choke out on a cough.

"I felt it." Jason answers my unfinished question. He looks at me and the high noon sun glints off tiny dew like droplets of water on his lashes. His hair and clothes are sodden, just like my own. He pushes a drenched lock of hair off my cheek. "I felt the power, but I also felt something else... something more, Kate."

I knew it. There was something more than just god-like power behind our efforts today. I feel like I'm starting to get used to what we're both capable of, what with all the crazy incidents that keep happening lately.

The warm feeling is also still there. Jason hasn't let go of my hand. We stand together in the water. I don't even care if the immersed half of my skin gets pickled beyond belief, all I want to do is be here with Jason right now, because I know he's going to kiss me. We are soaking wet. We just calmed possessed waters. I almost drowned, but none of that matters right now. All that's important is that I get the kiss I've been longing for. The kiss that I know is meant to be. Like fate has something interlocked with the importance of this kiss.

Any second now and our fates will be sealed—

"Kate!"

Someone screams my name.

"Kaaaaaaate!"

Someone is still screaming my name.

"Jaaaaaason! Kate!"

When that someone doesn't stop screaming either of our names, I'm forced to tear my concentration away from the blonde god before me.

"What are you guys doing?" Shana has entered the pool. She starts tugging at my arm.

The moment of our pre-destined kiss is lost forever. Jason nods knowingly at me, and then at Shana. "We better help," he says, now leading the way out of the pool.

Grudgingly, I wade through the water after him, Shana chattering with panicked words into my ear the entire time. "Did you see that crap at the bottom of my pool?" She questions. "What the hell happened?"

As water drips off me, splashing onto the cement patio, I turn to Shana who's now standing beside me. Even though I was overwhelmed by thoughts of smooching with Jason only a minute ago, the answer to her question comes to me. "It was a curse, Shana," I tell her. "And I know exactly who done it."

*

Familiar sounds of ambulance sirens wail in the distance. There are already a few paramedics who've arrived on the scene, and a lot of pool party goers have been escorted onto stretchers. Luckily no one drowned or got too water-logged by the cursed pool darkness. Unluckily though, Amelia's bikini top came off during the wet fracas and somehow I think she was faking being out of breath until Jason offered her a towel to cover up with.

I scowl at Amelia as she moans and groans while lying on a sun lounger. Funny how she'd refused to go with the first paramedic team who'd arrived on the scene. She's definitely making a scene now, vying for Jason's attention.

She doesn't get it though, because he turns quickly to me. "We have to reach Mount Olympus now, Kate."

Say what?

I stop scowling at Amelia and look up at him.

"This has to be your mother's doing."

Can he read my mind? I was just thinking... Wait. Why did Jason just say we need to get to Mount Olympus. "My mom is at home though."

He looks at me funny. "Not your mortal mother, Kate. We need to get to Mount Olympus to see your goddess mother, your *real* mother."

"Jason." I state his name flatly.

He picks up on my tone of voice. "I know you've been trying to avoid seeing the obvious, Kate." He takes my hand in his and a sensation of power warms my moist skin. There's also that other feeling that lies behind his touch. It's similar to god-like power, but there's something more there...

"Kate." Shana interrupts. "You guys can see the next paramedics, okay?"

I look at my best friend. She's drenched from head to toe and her eyes are pink. There's a worried look on her face and I don't think her eyes are sore from the chlorine water.

She's been crying.

"Shana!" Releasing Jason's hand —only slightly reluctantly— I wrap my arm around her shoulders. "You are the one who's going to see the paramedics right now."

Shana deflates into my arms. "This is all my fault, Kate. I don't know how this could have happened."

I knew it! She's feeling guilty for no reason. "Are you crazy? This wasn't your doing at all, Shana!" We've stopped walking along the grassy path through her back yard. Jason is following close behind.

"But everyone almost drowned at my party!" Shana wails, then immediately starts sobbing into her hands.

Jason steps forward. "Hey, listen," he says comfortingly. "Kate and I know exactly who did this, Shana, and we're leaving now to make sure nothing like this ever happens again. Right, Kate?"

He looks up at me with pleading eyes and I can no longer doubt him.

It's at this moment that I realize my own selfishness. I know that I'm the cause of all this chaos. The disaster that happened in the Underworld all those months ago. The swarm of bees blitzing out of the movie screen yesterday.

All my fault for the simple reason that I won't trust a god.

Why have I been fooling myself this entire time? How would I know who my real mother is? Just because I think I *feel* that my mother is Melanie Nicholls, doesn't mean it's true. Not if Jason — who just so happens to be an actual god— says it's not true.

If he's telling me, like he's been trying to tell me for a while now, that my real mother is a goddess of Mount Olympus, then I have to believe him.

Don't I?

If it means all these crazy curses stop happening then yes, I need to face the facts and own up.

"Shana." I put her at arm's length. "This isn't your fault, it's mine." I'm determined to do the right thing. "And I'm going to fix it, I promise."

My best friend immediately stops whimpering. "Somehow I totally believe you, Kate."

I look from her to Jason and back again, questioningly.

"Well, it's obvious that you mean what you say when you're determined to fix something." Now Shana is smiling. "You kicked ass in the Underworld, Kate. If you say you're going to fix whatever dark thing happened in my swimming pool, I believe you all the way!"

I return her smile. A paramedic sees to Shana, leaving Jason and I alone in the sunny garden.

"Are you ready to go?" He asks me.

I look at him sheepishly. "Are you asking me if I'm ready to go to the most powerful place known to exists? To Mount Olympus to see my real mother?"

Jason looks surprised. There's a smile in his eyes though and I think he's happy I've finally relented to his suggestions about my true parentage.

"Yeah, Jason, I'm very ready."

He nods knowingly at me and takes my hand. "Then let's go to limboland."

*

It's as though I don't even have to think about the limboland Jason mentioned before we're there.

I'm dry. Jason is dry. And we're both dressed up like lunatics. At least, I think my ensemble is insane. I'm standing on a cloud in the sky, because that's where limboland is. It's the place between the Underworld below and Mount Olympus; a floating island in the distance.

My ludicrous outfit is a dress. Flowing red velvet robes entwined with gold filigree stitching. Even my now dry hair has golden leaves running through it. There must be a fashion goddess, or a hair stylist entity floating around this realm, because every time I enter these places, my outer persona reflects an ancient mythological appearance.

Half my dark hair is piled on top of my head while the rest flows softly down my back.

"That dress suits you." Jason smiles at me. We're still holding hands.

"I gotta say," I wink at him, looking down at his legs, which are exposed below short white robes. "The gladiator-prince look really suits you."

"Are you making fun of me, Kate?" He continues to grin before yanking me close and wrapping an arm around my waist. "If we weren't in such a hurry, I'd show you what I do to those who dare to mock me."

My jaw drops open in mock surprise and I'm really wishing at this point that we weren't in such a rush. I wouldn't mind staying on a soft floating cloud with a god for a while. Especially a blonde god who I just so happen to be crushing on big time.

"Perhaps I'll show you later."

Those are Jason's final words to me before he whisks me into the air.

I don't have time to ponder his statement now. I'm too busy getting to grips with flying at high velocity. It's been a while since I've experienced such a thing, and my stomach seriously isn't in agreement with this aerial course of action.

By the time we land on Mount Olympus, I'm feeling woozy. "You could have warned me you were going to do that." We've touched down in the massive courtyard of a ludicrously majestic garden. There's a nearby marble bench that I immediately flop onto. "I'm not exactly used to flying without being contained inside an airplane, you know."

"Sorry, Kate, but needs must." Jason sits down next to me. "Now that you've accepted your mother is a goddess, you'll be able to do a lot more flying with me more often." Jason positively beams at me at this point.

"Are you crazy? There's no way I'm flying anywhere ever again."

Now he laughs. "Okay, let's stay here forever."

"What?" I'm taken aback briefly.

"Well," Jason fakes indifference with a grin still plastered on his face. "If you want to get back to the mortal realm, you'll have to fly with me to limboland first."

Slapping him playfully on the shoulder, I'm starting to get fed up with his happy skippy attitude. I suppose I can't blame the guy though. He's not just a regular teenager and I can see that coming home to Mount Olympus, his real home, totally cheers him up.

"Yeah, yeah. Whatever." I stand up, hoping to find renewed balance in my step.

"Whoa, hold on, Kate. Take it easy." Jason stands too and holds my elbow. "I was just joking, if you need to rest for a while, it's okay."

"I'm fine, let's just get this over with. If my mom really is a goddess, then I want to meet her." Steadying myself further, I glance around the garden fit for royalty. "I really need to ask her why she keeps trying to kill her own daughter!"

Jason doesn't look surprised at my outburst. Well, why would he?

After everything that's been inflicted upon me —upon us both— in the last few months, I have to wonder why my supposed parent keeps hurling all these curses my way. I know Jason must have been thinking the same thing this whole time.

"I wasn't going to say…" he pauses. "I didn't want it to be true, but I think you're right, Kate. I always hoped you'd meet your goddess mother someday, but I've been trying not to admit to myself that she's the one behind all these incidents. I'm sure there's a reason for it though, the gods work in mysterious ways sometimes. It's hard to know what a goddess might be planning. And the fact that your mother is a Fate really makes it all much more difficult to understand."

When I fail to respond with anything but silence for the next few seconds, Jason looks at me with concern. "Are you all right? Kate…? Kate?" He snaps his fingers in front of my eyes, and I snap back into reality.

"Did you just say my goddess mother is a Fate?"

Jason nods his head. He looks grateful that I've spoken coherently, but worried about his latest revelation. "Um, yes," he smiles nervously. "Your goddess mother is Clotho. She spins the threaded fate of mankind."

After hearing the words Jason just spoke, I really need to sit down again. Fortunately I don't need to find a bench to do so because I've already fallen onto my rear end with the shock of it all.

The grass I've immediately sat onto is soft. As soft as a cloud of limboland. My hands spread out into the velvety blades of greenest grass. I'm dazed, confused. I'm having trouble mentally digesting what Jason just told me about my goddess mother.

"Oh, Kate!" Jason has already sat down next to me. "I'm so sorry,

I thought you knew."

My face crumples and my upper lip curls. "You thought I knew that my goddess mother was a Fate? How the heck would I know that?"

"Well," Jason scoots closer to me until our skirts are touching. "I thought you speculated about it."

Now that I think about it, I decide he's right. But my thoughts don't add up to the conclusion that my mother is a Fate of Mount Olympus. The spinning of life-thread pings a strange connective thought in my mind, but I can't quite put my finger on what it is I'm contemplating.

"By the grace, your highness."

A man's voice grumbles above us and I look up. An old man dressed in elaborate flowing green robes looks down at us. And now he's looking up at us because he's just prostrated himself before Jason.

"Whoa, what the...?" Jason jumps to his feet. Bending over, he puts his hands under the man's shoulders and helps him to his feet. "Don't ever do that again, okay man?" Stepping back slightly, Jason runs a frustrated hand through his soft blonde hair.

"But, my lord!" The old man croons. "You are the new son of Zeus. I am honored beyond eternity to be blessed with your presence!"

Will wonders never cease around here? If I'm going to be meeting my Fate for a mother soon, I'm going to have to realize that I'm no longer on the planet Earth. I'm on the powerful plane of Mount Olympus. I'm going to have to get used to startling realizations without having to sit down all the time.

Finding a new resolve within myself, I stand up.

"And who is this beautiful princess?" The old man turns his

attentions to me. "Is she your betrothed?"

"Err..." I mumble at the same time Jason looks for the pockets of his nonexistent jeans to stuff his hands into.

What an awkward situation. First the old guy plants his face into the ground at Jason's feet, and now he's presuming way too much about whatever relationship the golden god and I might or might not have.

I really want to get out of here.

"We're here to see Clotho, my good sir." Jason speaks so eloquently to the old man. "Is she here?"

"Yes of course, master." The old guy bows and extends an arm. "She's at her loom."

Jason quickly takes my hand and we swiftly head in the direction the old man has indicated. "Where are we going, master?" I tease him.

"Don't you dare." Jason smiles as we hurry across the soft grass in our gladiator looking sandals.

Soon enough, a large square building comes into view. It has massive columns in front of the entrance and I'm reminded of the Acropolis in Athens, Greece. Even though this official Olympian version of the building is on a smaller scale, the structure is absolutely stunning. Everything around here is incredible to behold. We're in a place of ultimate power, I suppose buildings and homes would have to be amazing enough to appease the gods.

"Is this where my..." I can't bring myself to say the word 'mother' even if I've accepted the fact that the goddess in question truly is my real mom. "Is this Clotho's house?"

"Yep." Jason places his hand on the massive double door entrance, and they swing wide open.

"Um." I mumble, glancing inside. "Nice place."

I probably just uttered the understatement of the year. Not only was the exterior of this Fate's home impressive, but the interior is even more so. As Jason and I make our way indoors, I'm astounded by the majesty surrounding me.

There are glowing, sparkling curtains dangling everywhere in this vast marble room. Upon closer inspection I can see that they aren't curtains which flow from high ceiling to floor, but thousands upon thousands of strands of light.

Jason pulls me along the stone floor and I dare to run my hands along the soft hanging tendrils. "Are these...?" I gasp when a tingling sensation flutters through my fingertips. "Are these threads of life?"

"Of course they are," Jason whispers almost sacredly, as though we're in a holy place or something. I do kind of feel like being reverent around all these life-threads. They just seem so vulnerable all hanging here out in the open...

"Be careful! You don't want to break any of these strands, Kate. You could kill someone!"

Gasping, I jump back and pull my hand away from the threads. When I turn toward Jason, I find he's giggling behind his free hand that's plastered over his mouth.

"You dork!" I shout, no longer caring about reverence. "Don't scare me like that!"

"What?" Jason's reply is to moan at me. "I was just joking, Kate. Only the three Fates can cut a mortal's life-thread."

"That's not quite true, my young lord."

My head snaps to the right at the sound of a woman's voice.

"Clotho." Jason clears his throat as though nervous. "I... umm...

brought Kate here to introduce the two of you."

The Fate smiles kindly. She has long, curly blonde hair entwined with tiny daisies. Her flowing white robes are elaborately held together by golden ropes at her waist and shoulders.

I don't know what to say and I'm guessing neither does she because neither of us speaks.

Jason interrupts the silence by clearing his throat again. "What did you mean I wasn't quite right?"

Clotho wanders over to the nearest curtain of life-thread strands. As she nears them they begin to glow even brighter. She doesn't even have to reach for the tendrils, as soon as the Fate lifts her fingers, three strands of life float through the air and then settle into her palm.

She moves toward us and I'm mesmerized by the threads of life she holds in her hand.

"I suppose this day had to come eventually." Clotho sighs and takes my hand from Jason's. She places the life strands into my palm. The brightness the tendrils displayed upon the Fates own touch, doesn't fade once they're in my grasp. "Kate," she says to me. "You do have the power to cut these cords, but do you have the will to end a mortal's life?"

Before I know what's happening, a pair of very shiny scissors are flashed in front of my face. Balking at the traumatic situation, I back away, dropping the strands of life in the process.

"What are you saying, lady? Don't be asking me to murder some person on Earth, okay?"

Clotho laughs. "You are your mother's daughter, Kate Nicholls." She stretches out her fingers and the strands of life float up into her hand.

I'm wondering what she's talking about, and if the goddess of mortal fate is in her right mind. I glance at Jason who shrugs his shoulders. Great, well he's no help. I'm starting to wish he hadn't brought me here at all.

"What do you know of these life-threads, Kate?" Clotho moves toward me again. "This one, for example," with a flick of her finger one of the glowing strands of light floats into the air. It hovers there, squirming slowly like a long sparkling worm. "It belongs to a human who suffers greatly, inflicted with disease. This man's life is a misery, Kate. He longs to escape his existence so vehemently that he's even attempted suicide on two occasions." She looks at me with cold, gray eyes. "Would you deny him the bliss of death, Kate? Would you end his suffering if you knew him? If you knew what true pain was?"

"Leave the girl alone, Clotho. She doesn't understand your work." The Fate looks embarrassed when a man enters the room. He has wavy black hair as dark as the short robes he wears. Slowly, he comes toward Clotho. "Eighteen mortal years have passed for her." He croons in her ear. "It's her entire life time, up till now, and I think she deserves to know the truth."

Relenting, Clotho waves her fingers. All three of the life-strands float away, re-attaching themselves to one of the main curtains.

"Yeah," Jason grumbles. "I didn't bring Kate here to be mentally and morally questioned. I brought her here to learn about her real mother."

Clotho looks at the man. "Titus?"

Like Jason did mere moments ago, the man Titus shrugs his shoulders questioningly. "Her real mother, you say?"

"Yes!" Jason looks impatient now. "Clotho." He points to the

Fate. "You're her real goddess mother."

Titus and Clotho both frown at him. "No, I'm not. Melanie Nicholls is her mother."

"What...?" Jason looks confused now. "But what about her powers?"

"I gave the power of the Fates to your mother, Kate." Clotho cuddles closer to the man, who I assume is her husband, or something. "She was the one who helped Titus and the others escape Tartarus."

Jason takes a step back. Seemingly out of nowhere, he's drawn a great gleaming sword. The blade of which is in the shape of a lightning bolt. "You're him." He mutters. "You're the Titus my father warned me about."

"Whoa." I blurt. "Where the heck did you get that thing?"

I don't get an answer from Jason because the next thing I know, the great sky light above *cracks* with a thunderous *boom*.

Clotho screams and Titus pulls her aside. Before I know what's happening, I too am pushed out of the way. It's a good thing Jason stepped up when he did, because a sheet of glass falls from above, crashing into the very place where I was standing.

Shards blast at my feet. I turn, blocking my face with my arms. A great booming voice rings out when the final spray of glass settles. "My newest son has drawn his sword of defense, Titus. I know you are here. Show yourself!"

Zeus.

Jason's dad is here.

When I turn back around, my fears are confirmed. Standing atop a broken dome ceiling that's now lying on the floor in the center of this massive room, is the king of the gods.

The reason I'm fearful of this all powerful being, isn't because I'm worried he's going to plant his noggin onto one of my shoulders. He's already done that to me before. Nope, the reason I'm now backing away, crunching my gladiator sandals over broken glass, is because the god of gods is aiming his sparking lightning bolt of fury straight at me.

"What are you doing, father?" Jason steps in front of me. I peek around his shoulder and I can see that the great white bearded Zeus is still holding tightly to his electrified bolt of lightning.

"Stand aside, son." Zeus' voice booms. "Kate will reveal her father's whereabouts to me now."

"My dad?" I cringe at the anger in the king's voice. "He's at work." Fumbling through my velvet skirts, I search for my cell phone. "I think I've got his office number—"

"SILENCE!"

Bang!

Zeus has just shot a great big hole in a giant pillar, by use of his crackling lightning bolt. Rocks spray everywhere and a great plume of marble dust blasts me off my feet. I fall back as though in slow motion and I'm fully expecting to crack my butt bone on the hard floor any nano-second now...

No breaking of bum occurs. I land with a soft plonk onto billowing cloud. When the dust of the pillar explosion settles, I can see that it's cloud vapor drifting away from my line of vision.

Holy moly. I'm in limboland.

Scrambling to my feet, pushing cloud fluff aside, I glance around. "How the...? How did I get here?" I cry out loud.

"We brought you here."

Turning around swiftly causes the bottom of my robe style dress to swirl the misty clouds at my ankles.

Clotho and Titus are here. "What's going on?" I blurt and stamp my foot, causing yet more cloud to puff and billow. "Why did Zeus almost strike me with a bolt of lightning back there?" I point toward the floating island of Mount Olympus in the distance. "And where is Jason?"

Instead of answering any of my questions, both Titus and Clotho look down.

"Hey," I say irritably, snapping my fingers to get their attention. "Don't even think about trying to escape into the Underworld down there. How did the two of you get here to limboland anyway?"

Finally, someone answers me. Clotho keeps her eyes on her feet when she speaks though. "This is the gateway between realms, Kate. And if you want to know where your boyfriend is, I suggest you look down."

"My boy..." What's she talking about? Jason isn't my boyfriend. Is he? Well, I want him to be... Oh my hell! Why is my mind wandering at a time like this? Frustration bangs back into my thoughts. I'm so confused I can't even concentrate on the immediate situation. "I told you the Underworld is down there!"

Stomping through cloud mist, I float/walk my way towards the Fate and Titus. Following their gazes, I tip my head down. What I see below the clouds isn't the Underworld, like I was expecting. What I'm seeing makes my heart almost stop beating inside my chest.

My mother is down there. I'm looking at a vision of our house. My father is there too and so is Jason, and so is Zeus.

Zeus and his stupid lightning bolt that he's pointing straight at my dad's head.

"We have to get down there!" I scream. "Zeus is going to blow up my dad's head!"

"You can take us there, Kate." Clotho kneels down in the cloud beside me. "Just concentrate on—"

I don't even hear the rest of her words. I've concentrated all right. My thoughts are so swift that we're in the living room of my house within a split second.

"Kate!" Mom yells the moment I appear with Clotho and Titus beside me.

"Jason!" I shout at the guy who still has a lightning bolt shaped sword in his hand. "Tell your dad to let my dad go right now!"

"I can hear you perfectly well, Kate. There's no need for my son to relay any information to me." Zeus practically rolls his eyes at me. "And as for releasing your father. I'll do no such thing until things have been explained to me. Like what you're doing out of Tartarus." He grips my dad's neck a little tighter, causing my father to gurgle.

"It's not Rasmun's fault, Zeus!" Titus steps forward. "It was my idea. I asked him to help release the Titans from Tartarus when he found Melanie."

What the heck is that Titus dude talking about?

"The Titans just want to live amongst the mortals peacefully." Clotho speaks up. "None of the elder gods would ever try to overthrow Olympus."

Of all the confusing things the gods are now saying, the strangest reaction is when Zeus starts laughing. "So this is where the Titans escaped to? And you expect me to believe that none of them are planning a coup of Mount Olympus?"

"It's true, my lord." Mom steps forward, addressing Zeus. "The Titans have been living amongst us in peace for many years now."

"Besides," Clotho adds. "If you do anything to Rasmun, I'll be forced to cut your thread of existence." She twirls her fingers through the air and a life-thread appears. It floats before us all, but it's golden in hue, unlike the bright white tendrils I saw on Mount Olympus.

"Is that what I think it is?" I mumble.

"Clotho!" Jason steps between her and his father, jagged edged sword raised. "What are you doing?"

"Well!" The Fate huffs as the life-thread continues to wiggle in the air. "If Zeus is going to threaten a demi god and all the Titans, I have to do *something* about it!"

Underneath his big white beard, Zeus' cheeks are bright pink with anger. He watches Clotho as she produces a flashing silver pair of scissors from beneath the folds of her robes.

Looking down at my red velvet gown, I'm suddenly wondering why I'm still dressed like this in the mortal realm. Jason's still garbed in his gladiator short skirt too. Normally this ancient apparel only appears when we're in realms of power.

"How?" Zeus now asks only one word as he releases my dad.

"Rasmun!" Mom yells and throws her arms around Dad's neck.

"Why does everyone keep calling you that?" I shout at my father.

Actually, a lot of shouting ensues at this point. Zeus is shouting at Clotho and Titus. I'm shouting at my parents who are shouting back at me and nothing is getting explained very well.

"Shut up!" Jason shouts louder than us all. He waves his gleaming sword up over his head and brings it down in a glistening arch, fully slicing Mom's new couch in two.

"Holy shit!"

"Kate!" Mom glares at me.

"What?" I gape at her. "He just cut the whole sofa in half!"

"Oh jeez." Jason cringes. "I'm really sorry about that." He sheaths his sword through an invisible holster at his waist and the lightning rod blade vanishes. "I just want to know what's going on."

No one says anything and then—

Clap!

Dad bangs his hands together. He keeps them there and a rumbly noise happens in the couch. The two dissected pieces smash together and stich themselves up with a glowing golden seam, straight down the middle of the cushions.

My jaw drops open in astonishment. "How the...?" I exclaim.

"You're a Titan." Jason's statement isn't a question for my father.

"It's the truth, Kate," my dad says. I look at him in his dark business suit. He runs a hand through his hair that's the exact shade as my own, except mine doesn't have gray running through it at the temples.

Mom cuddles close to Dad. "We never thought we'd have to tell you, Kate, but you're half demi god."

"That's what you said I was." I turn to Jason.

Grumble.

This from Zeus, who I eyeball for a second.

"Are you going to listen?" Clotho edges her sharp looking scissors closer toward Zeus' life-strand.

The god of Mount Olympus doesn't answer her, but he does grunt again, as though annoyed.

"Yeah." Jason looks stunned. "I thought you were a demi god because Clotho was your goddess mother."

The Fate in question shakes her head. "No, I'm not her mother. I gave the power of the Fates to your mortal mother, Kate. When your father—"

I cut her off mid-sentence. "Dad? Your real name isn't Richard?"

"No, darling." He answers me with an honest look in his eyes. "My true name is Rasmun."

"Shall I continue?" Clotho looks irritated by my interruption.

"By all means." If it's possible to wave your hand sarcastically, this is totally what Zeus does, before folding his arms once again. "Enlighten us with your stories, Fate."

Clotho squints evilly at Zeus, but continues. "When Rasmun found Melanie, Titus discovered she was the one of her generation who could access the realm between."

I assume she's talking about limboland, but I'm not going to interrupt her again to ask.

"Titus told Rasmun to ask Melanie if she would help the Titans escape an eternity in Tartarus, the land beneath even the Underworld. Rasmun did not agree to ask for Melanie's help for ages."

Clotho looks at my dad with a peevish face. What's that all about?

"I didn't want her to think I was using her for the gain of our kind." Dad returns Clotho's glare.

"Yes… well," she mumbles. "You weren't without your one true love for millennia as I was."

"Titus!" Jason suddenly yells. "Father, you were right, Clotho did hook up with Titus thousands of years ago."

Zeus simply nods at his hot blonde son. I can't help getting distracted by the sight of Jason in that gladiator suit. With all this talk of love in the room, I'm becoming overwhelmed by the story that's being revealed. I have to admit, Jason wowed me big time when he held that gleaming sword in his hand.

Snapping back into reality, I realize Clotho is explaining things again.

"You knew of my love for him?" She asks Zeus. "And yet you still cast Titus into Tartarus." Clotho slices at the air next to Zeus' still floating life-thread. "I should cut this right now!"

"Clotho," Titus places his hands gently onto the Fate's arm. "I'm here now. Rasmun is with Melanie and all the Titans have been freed. What's important is that Zeus understands our desire to remain, without fear of harm." He looks to the god of Olympus and then to my mother. "You were given the power of the Fates to help with freeing us from Tartarus. I have thanked you many times, but let me thank you now, once again."

"Wait just a gosh darn minute." Stepping forward, something pings in my mind. "You have powers of the Fates?"

Mom nods her head.

"And dad is a demi god?"

He nods his head.

"That's why you have powers too, Kate." Jason interjects.

This time, I nod my head at him in confirmation that his statement must be correct. That's not what's niggling at the back of my brain though.

"Mom," I say flatly. "You've been sabotaging my dates!"

Mom looks guilty-faced. "I'm sorry about that, Kate. I didn't know about the consequences until today."

"You mean...?"

"Yep," I answer Jason. "You used your powers in your glowing sewing machine room. Right, Mom?"

This is what dawned on me. I remembered the glowing light from beneath the door in my mom's office. I remember how her voice had sounded like it was coming from upstairs, how she'd tricked me into not going into that room. Now that all this magical ability has been revealed, I've figured her out.

"People got stung, Mom!"

"Oh my." Clotho looks surprised.

"I know, honey!" Mom loses it. "I've repaired the damages done. That's what I was doing when you saw the light coming from beneath the door. I knew you were there, so I tried to make it seem like I was upstairs."

"Melanie." Dad shakes his head.

"Well!" Suddenly, Mom looks put out. "I didn't know what else to do! We couldn't just let our daughter date a god of Olympus!"

Everyone starts yelling at each other again.

"What's wrong with her dating my son?" Zeus grumbles.

"We didn't want you finding out about the Titans." Clotho threatens with his life-thread again.

"Yeah, what's wrong with me?"

My heart leaps into my eyes nearly spilling forth as tears when Jason asks this question.

"Shut up, everyone!" This time it's my turn to yell. And thankfully, all the gods and goddesses and demi gods in the room go quiet.

"Jason, there's nothing wrong with you and there's definitely nothing wrong with dating you either." I glare at my mother. "If you married a demi god, then I get to date one too."

There. I've made my statement and my parents are just going to have to deal with it.

"And no more plagues on my friends!" I add.

"All right, Kate." Mom relents. "I honestly fixed everyone who got stung or water-logged."

I'm surprised at Mom's apology, so I don't really know what else to say. I don't really have to do or say anything though, because Zeus grabs everyone's attention when he stands, shuffles over to Clotho and takes her scissors from her. With a flick of his wrist he juts the scissors into the air and up through the middle of his own life-thread, cutting the glowing tendril in two, just as easily as Jason had sliced through our entire sofa only moments before.

The fact that Zeus hasn't dropped dead proves that he knew what he was doing when he cut his own strand of life.

"You knew I was bluffing." Clotho purses her lips shut after speaking.

"I knew you were bluffing and that you did not create a life-thread for me." Zeus puts his fists on his hips. "I am the god of Olympus. Strands of life can only be created for mortals. If I had truly believed the Titans were a threat, I would have wiped them all out the moment I arrived here."

I guess time can soften even a god's heart. I don't know much about whatever wars were fought between the Titans and the Olympians, like thousands of years ago, but I guess even beings with power have to keep up with mortal times. And there sure is a lot of love to go around these days.

There's a lot of love right here in our house. Dad the demi god and his love for Mom the mortal with new powers of the Fates. Titus and his love for the goddess Clotho. Even Zeus loves his wife Hera. After all, the two of them attached their heads to my shoulders just a few months ago. Despite the fact that it was a horrifying time for me, at least I know they worked together as a husband and wife team.

Zeus' warning about wiping out all the Titans hangs on the air, making the situation socially awkward, even though no one's in a choke-hold.

"So that's why everyone is so accepting about the gods in this town!" I can't help myself from blurting this out. "Everyone is a god around here!"

"Well," Dad clears his throat nervously. "Not everyone. Some are demi gods, there are goddesses too. But most of your friends parents are Titans, Kate."

"Wow." This is overwhelming stuff. I need to sit down and I do so on the previously sliced sofa. "Things are going to be different around here now, aren't they?" I ask Jason when he sits next to me.

"Probably," he replies. "But in a good way."

"Really?" Turning my head, I look at him. "How?"

"Because I get to date you now, Kate." Jason leans forward and tucks his hand gently behind my ear, cupping my cheek in his palm. He pulls me close and presses his lips to mine.

Finally! I get kiss from the god I dared to date. I'm on the ground in a normal realm, but my heart feels as though it's soaring through the clouds.

STORY III

Gorgon Cursed

The last time I took part in a high school event I'd poisoned everyone and all the guest had ended up in the Underworld. Needless to say, I've had nothing to do with organizing tonight's dance. It was all put together by my best friend Shana.

Okay so maybe I'm slightly exaggerating.

It wasn't actually me who'd poisoned everyone at the Death by Chocolate fundraiser event, and it also wasn't my own powers that had sent all the visitors to the Underworld. That had been the work of Zeus and Hera and right now I just want to forget about it.

Tonight I'm at a dance with the god of my dreams and I'm going to enjoy myself. "So soft," I say, tousling Jason's blonde hair. "Are you using some kind of ambrosia shampoo of the gods?"

My deity boyfriend laughs. "No, I'm not. And don't do that, you're going to mess up my do." He smiles.

I laugh and pull my hands (regrettably) free from his luscious locks. The slow song ends and it's replaced by a tune with a fast beat. "Ooh! I love this song!" I throw my hands into the air and start shaking my booty double-time to the new PSY song

Jason joins me, but I'm thinking he's wishing the slow jams would come back on. That is if I'm judging by the way he keeps trying to bump-and-grind with me.

"Mato fato gentleman." I sing and snap my fingers nerdily, and I just don't care.

"That's not how the song goes, Kate. May I cut in?"

Who the...? What the...? Who the heck said that and how did I hear them so easily over the throbbing music?

Ceasing all gyrating activities, Jason and I both stop dancing.

Apparently it was Amelia who'd uttered those old-school words of her's. I mean seriously, she's asking to cut in as though she's some sort of twenties gentleman getting ready to cut his/her rug?

"What do you want, Amelia?" I scowl at her.

In my opinion I find it (sarcastically) hilarious how the head cheerleader here at Lakepoint High, doesn't have an accent when she's screaming away doing cheers, but when she's trying to come-on to someone else's boyfriend she has a certain way of flicking her auburn hair and putting on her foreign accent.

"I would like to dance with Jason." She replies flatly.

"Oh would you—"

I don't get to finish my rhetorical question because my godly BF has just stepped between us. "I'd love to dance with you, my lady." He takes Amelia's hand in his own and together they glide away.

I'm standing here like I've just literally been sucker punched in the gut. Is this some kind of sick joke, or did my mighty Mount Olympus boyfriend just totally ditch me on the dance floor?

"This can't be happening." Balling my fists, I stomp forward. My frisky A-line dress flaps around my thighs. I tap Jason's shoulder. "What do you think you're doing?" I frown at him.

"I'm dancing, of course."

Flabbergasted. That is 100% me right now.

"Yeah, I can see you're dancing." My face is starting to hurt. It's becoming so red with fury I can see the scarlet color dancing before my eyes. "But why in hades are you dancing with her?"

Jason's reply surprises me. "I don't know."

I glance at Amelia who's smirking from ear to ear. "Maybe he just wants to dance with someone who knows how to do it right, Kate."

I don't like the way she's just said my name, not even for one second. And I definitely don't like the way the two of them are dancing together. It's like they're waltzing together or something. Well, they would be if I weren't blocking their dance path at every step.

"Shoo." Amelia dares? She just shooed me with a wave of her hand. "Don't butt in, Kate, or you'll regret it."

Oh will I? Somehow I doubt it.

"I think..." Jason is mumbling something. "I think... I don't feel so good."

I knew it. Something must be wrong with my (incredibly handsome, yet really in trouble for leaving me) boyfriend. Especially if he's actually choosing to dance with the enemy.

"Tell Kate to back off, Jason." When Amelia says this she has the nerve to wrap her arms around *my* boyfriend's neck.

That red-anger I thought I saw earlier actually flames into my vision. I'm so mad I'm not even aware of all the other teenagers dancing around in the school gym. Placing my hands onto Amelia's, I wrench them off Jason's shoulders. "You're the one who needs to back off, you b—"

Her eyes light up.

I'm not talking about her retinas lighting up with love as she continues to gaze at my BF. I mean they are literally dancing with light. It's a light that zips and zings around her irises and sparks out the corners of her eyes.

"What the?" Jason starts backing away from Amelia.

"Oh so you've finally realized you should be dancing with me and not her?" I should probably be more concerned with the fact that the girl's eyes are glowing, but right now I'm still hot in the face with anger about my boyfriend's dance floor betrayal.

"What's up with her eyes?" Jason looks worried.

"How should I know? You're the one who was all up and close with her, why don't you ask—"

"Umm, Kate... I don't think now's the time to—"

Flash!

All the light from Amelia's stormy eyes erupts straight into my own.

"I'm blind!" I scream as someone grabs me around my middle.

"Whooooo, whoa!" I hear Jason yell before the pressure around my waist vanishes.

"What's going on?" My hands are splayed and I drop to my knees, feeling along the floor. Around me the music cuts off and teenagers are screaming. When my hand finds purchase on someone's heeled foot, my vision starts to clear.

Looking up and up I meet the gaze of Amelia's eyes. They're no longer lit up with light, so where is that glowing stream coming from?

"Oh no!" I scream and sit back onto my butt — hard. I've just noticed my reflection in the nearby window. It's my eyes that are now glowing! And not only that, my hair is brightening too. "What's happening to my hair?"

Amelia starts laughing. "It's already happened!"

She's right. Now I know why everyone has run away screaming. They've all backed away from me because my hair is no longer hair at all...

It's turned into tendrils of squirming snakes!

"Jason, help me!" Like the snakes that ooze from my scalp, I writhe on the floor. I'm completely grossed out by my reflection, so I turn away from the window and jump to my feet. "Where's Jason?" I point a stabby finger at Amelia.

Suddenly, the same finger shifts and it becomes a squirming snake, just like the ones on my head.

"Argh!" I scream and shake out my whole hand. When I look again my snake finger is back to its normal human shape. "What's happened to me?" I screech.

"I put the gorgon curse on you!" Amelia looks positively gleeful as she mocks me endlessly. "And you can stay like a snake lady until you tell me how to get to Mount Olympus.

By now, everyone in the gymnasium has left the dance entirely. The only person who comes to my rescue is Shana. Although, the closer she gets to me, the more I think she's recognizing what's attached to my scalp.

"Oh my... Kate!" Shana's eyes go wide with fear. "Your hair... it's... it's..."

"It's like a reverse snake pit!" Amelia laughs again.

I'm too freaked out to respond right now. I can feel the snakes tugging at my flesh where my hair follicles used to be. I catch many of the writhing forms in my peripheral vision, and it makes me want to close my eyes forever.

"What are you laughing at?" Shana finally dares to approach. "This isn't funny, we have to help her!"

"She's not going to help me!" This time I don't point a finger at Amelia because I'm afraid it will turn into a snake again. I simply jut my head in her general direction. "She's the one who cursed me!"

"She what?" Shana explodes. "You what?" She turns to Amelia and punches her in the face.

Oh, wow, that was interesting. "Put my best friends hair back to normal right now."

"Ow!" Amelia has grabbed her nose. A trickle of blood oozes out from underneath. "You broke my nose!"

"I'm going to break your whole face if you don't undo whatever it is you did to Kate!"

Shana's on a roll and I'm not going to be the one to stop her.

"You'll regret this." Amelia says. She's not laughing now. "If you won't take me to Mount Olympus you're never going to see Jason again."

Why does she want to get to Mount Olympus so badly? I can't concentrate with these stupid snakes writhing around on my head and the only person —who isn't a mere person rather than a god— who can help me is gone.

Wait a second…

"Why do you want me to take you to Mount Olympus? Is that where Jason is? How did he get there?" Questions are firing from my mouth now that I'm somewhat getting used to my snake filled noggin. "Oh my word! Did you send Jason to Mount Olympus, Amelia?"

"Duh!" Her voice sounds nasally in reply, probably because she has to pinch her nose shut to keep it from bleeding out. It's funny because even though she had the power to curse me with snake hair, this annoying girl doesn't even have the ability to avoid a nose bleed after a much deserved punch in the nostrils by my best friend. "Of course I sent him there! I've got new powers now that I've realized my parents are gods. So I should be the one who's dating a god,

Kate. Not you!"

I smack my forehead in disgust. A head-snake bites my finger, so I pull my hand quickly away.

"So you've kidnapped my best friend's boyfriend and turned her hair into snakes?" Shana looks pissed. "You've got to the count of three to bring him back and undo the snake curse, or the punching is going to start all over again."

"I don't think so."

Poof!

Amelia disappears in a puff of smoke.

*

"Ouch!" I'm at home now —in Mom's sewing room— and she's pulling at one of the sakes on my head with an actual comb. "That hurts."

"Well, I guess cutting the snakes off isn't going to work," Dad says. I watch as he places a pair of Mom's razor sharp scissors onto a worktable. I'm not sure if they're Mom's sewing scissors or if they're super-powered blades from Mount Olympus. After all, my mom does possess the powers of the Fates.

"Dad!" I yell. "You weren't seriously going to cut the snakes off, were you?"

"That would have made a bloody mess." Shana cringes and frankly so do I.

"No," Mom glares at my father. "Of course he wasn't going to cut the snakes off, dear."

"Just trying to lighten the mood." Dad puts his hands up in surrender and I'm wondering how he can possibly think this is the right time for jokes.

"You're trying to lighten the mood by making Kate think about ripping snakes off her head so that their guts and entrails—"

"Shana!" I wail in protest at her graphic explanations.

"What?" She shrugs. "It's true, that's what would happen if the snakes were cut off. There would be guts everywhere and—"

"Shana!" This time it's both Mom and Dad who silence her.

"Sorry." My best friend goes quiet.

"Now," Mom starts pacing the room. "We have to make sure Zeus doesn't find out about this."

Mom's right. My parent's relationship with the almighty Zeus isn't exactly a stable one. My dad is a Titan god and he had some help escaping Tartarus without Zeus knowing. I mean, Zeus obviously knows now. The Olympian god knows that the populace of this entire town mostly consists of Titan gods. He didn't send them back to Tartarus a few months ago and if he finds out what Amelia did to my hair…

I shudder to think my parents could both be sent back to the place that's beneath even the Underworld.

"What has that girl done?" I'm pretty sure Mom is referring to Amelia as she continues to pace the floor.

"She turned Kate's hair into snakes so she could have her boyfriend!" Shana is playing with the ends of her blonde hair.

"So she discovered her powers and this is what she decides to do with them?" Mom looks surprised. I can't say I'm shocked. I've always known Amelia was a skeez.

"Is it Amelia's dad who's a Titan, or her mom?" I'd love to be able to twirl my own hair —like Shana's doing— while I contemplate, but I fear doing so would get me a lost fingertip due to snake bite.

Mom stops pacing and her and Dad look at each other.

"Neither," Mom says. "Amelia's mother is Medusa.

"What?" Shana and I both screech at the same time.

"Medusa!" I cry. "That's what I'm like! My hair is snakes, just like hers'. So why aren't you guy's turning to stone when I look at you?"

"Relax, honey!" Dad places his hand on my shoulder, but then quickly pulls it away when one of my cranial snakes snaps at him. "You're not Medusa, you've just been unfortunately inflicted with the gorgon part of her curse. At least, that's what you told us Amelia said, right?"

I nod, causing the snakes on my head to twist and writhe. "She did curse me and I want these stupid things gone!" I'm surprised I haven't lost it before now. Why didn't the name of Medusa even cross my mind until Mom mentioned it? I guess it's because actually having snakes on your hair is quite distracting.

"I'll just go get my sword." Dad heads toward the door.

"You'll do no such thing, Richard, get back here," Mom demands.

"But we need to chop off our daughter's head." When Dad makes this statement of his it's as though the snakes have magically disappeared from my head. I'm so not aware of their presence in light of the fact that it would seem my own father wants to kill me.

"Don't be crazy, that won't work with Kate, she's not a full goddess of Mount Olympus!" Mom rages.

"Oh." Dad looks thoughtful. "I guess you're right. Chopping her head off might kill her for real."

"Wait." Shana speaks for the first time in a while. I'm glad she's piping up because I certainly can't seem to find my voice at the moment, due to the shocking conversation that's now occurring. "What are you guys talking about?"

"Medusa was cursed," Mom says. "But the curse was lifted when Perseus chopped off her gorgon head and her normal head grew back."

"It grew back?" Shana seems mystified.

"Well," Mom replies. "It didn't actually grow, her normal head just sort of reappeared because she was a goddess of Mount Olympus."

I glare at my father. "So you thought you could chop off my head just now, and my snake-less noggin would magically reappear as normal?"

"Well, yes." Dad looks at me as though to say *'why not?'* with a shrug of his shoulders.

"Oh, Dad." I sigh in despair. He really is a Titan god, and he needs to start learning the ways of mortals a lot better. Especially if my survival depends on it.

"So Medusa is Amelia's mother?" Shana starts chewing worriedly on the ends of her hair. If I did that my snake hair would actually bite back. "No wonder she's such a—"

"What did you say?" I interrupt my best friend because I suddenly can't hear her due to the fact that all the snakes on my head have started hissing like crazy.

"Here, honey," Mom says. "Let me see if I can help." She goes into the back room and comes out with an antique hand-held spool. A spool made of gold, inlaid with intricate designs.

It's her spool of the Fates.

Dad and Shana look on as I grab a freestanding mirror off the nearby table. "What are you going to do, Mom?" I look up at her from my seat. I'm a little worried after Dad's crazy chopping-off-my-head-with-sword idea, but then I realize Mom's the sensible one in this relationship.

"Trust me," is all she says before getting down to business.

She raises the golden spool up over my head and I watch in amazement as the magical tool gathers the life-strands of each of the snakes attached to my cranium. Mom makes a jerking motion and all of a sudden every snake on my head goes rigid.

"Oh great." I gasp, staring at my reflection. "So now I've got snake-spike hair?"

It's true. Every snake on my head is now standing straight out from my scalp. My head is one big snake sphere.

"I'm not done yet." Mom takes a nearby sheaf of floaty pink fabric from her desk and wraps it around my spike-snake-hair. The snakes squash down, she ties it expertly and now I'm wearing a turban.

"You'll never get away with that look at school." Shana stifles a laugh.

"I think we should try out my plan of chopping off her head." Dad doesn't even pretend not to laugh, he just burst out guffawing.

I'm starting to wish the other part of the gorgon curse wasn't left out of the spell that Amelia inflicted me with, because I would *so totally* turn my Dad and my best friend into statues —with my eyes— if I could right now.

*

"Kate, you can't take Amelia to Mount Olympus."

Shana and I are alone now, in my room, and she's trying to convince me not to do what I'm about to do.

"But you heard what she said, Shana. If I don't take her there I'll never see Jason again. Who knows what she's done with him?" I throw my hands up in the air. I don't know what else she expects me to do. I've got a head full of snakes under this pink turban and it totally doesn't match the outfit I've changed into.

Shana has borrowed some of my casual clothes so we're not

wearing the dresses we had on at the dance any more.

"If you take Amelia to Mount Olympus through limboland, I'll tell your parents on you, Kate."

"Oh that's real mature, Shana." She's going to tattle on me? "Maybe if you had snake-hair you'd see things my way."

"Look, Kate. Your mom said her and your dad are talking to Clotho the goddess—"

"Fate." I interrupt.

"What?"

"Clotho is a Fate, not a normal Olympian goddess."

"Whatever! Kate, your mom said for us to stay here while her and your dad communicate with Clotho about your hair!"

"Well maybe if I bring Amelia here first you can just punch her in the face until she changes my hair back!"

Shana looks thoughtful. "Actually, that's not a bad idea."

Huffing in exasperation, I stomp out of my bedroom. "I was just kidding about the punching. You can't beat Amelia up or she'll never tell us what she's done with Jason."

"Oh yeah." Shana follows me down the hall. "I forgot about her stupid threat."

"Well I remembered, and that's why I have to take her to Mount Olympus." Without waiting for Shana to reply, I head out the front door. Even if she can't adequately cover for me —when my parents discover I'm gone— they won't risk pursuing me to Mount Olympus because then Zeus will find out. The only thing I can do right now is what Amelia demanded.

Both luckily and unfortunately, Amelia lives next door to Shana. Lucky, because I know where I can find her, and unfortunate because she lives so close to my best friend.

When I arrive at Amelia's house —well, her parent's house, that is— every window is as dark as the night sky.

How can that crazy girl be asleep right now? I guess it's fine for her. I'm the one she cursed, and Jason is the one she banished to who knows where. I wouldn't be surprised if the evil harridan is sleeping like a baby despite the catastrophe she's caused to my hair!

Well, I won't stand for it. The snakes may be subdued and no longer writhing and hissing atop my head, but I still have to wear this ugly make-shift turban in public.

I throw a rock at Amelia's bedroom window.

And the window cracks.

"Oops." I tell myself before running away and hiding in some bushes.

"Who's out there?" The sensor porch light comes on as Amelia's mother, wrapped in a robe, opens the front door.

Through the shrubbery I can see her face and I try to picture her features surrounded by a halo of snakes, instead of the shiny long blonde hair on her head.

So that's Medusa. She must be absolutely obsessed with her hair now that it isn't in fact made of slithering serpents. I promise myself to take much better care of my own locks, should I ever be successful at getting Amelia to remove this horrific gorgon curse from my head.

After looking out into the night for a few minutes, Medusa goes back inside and shuts the door.

Now how am I supposed to get Amelia's attention? I can't just ring the doorbell. Her mother would ask so many questions that I really don't think Amelia wants her to know the answers to. Besides, her mother might have had her snaky head cut off, but that doesn't mean a guaranteed personality change. For all I know Amelia's mom could still retain a gorgon's attitude towards midnight interruptions, which is probably not a kind one, I'm sure.

"About time you showed up."

Amelia.

She's just come out from her back yard.

I punch my way through the bushes and dust off my jeans with two hands.

"Nice turban." Amelia adds, sarcastically.

I'm not going to give her the satisfaction of gloating by saying anything in response.

"Let's just go so you can take this stupid curse off my head."

"Yes." Amelia scowls. "Let's."

"Give me your hand." I extend my own.

"You're not going to try any tricks, are you?" She pauses, hand already half way stretched out to meet mine.

"No, Amelia. I'm not one for dirty tricks. I'm not like you in the slightest."

She actually smiles in response. "You just don't get it do you? I'm not doing this because I take pleasure in it, Kate. I'm doing it for the greater good."

She what now?

"Don't you get it?" The girl glares at me. "Jason and I are much better suited to each other. We'd make a stunning high school couple that would really motivate students—"

"Seriously? You're actually justifying your actions with that analogy?" I'm suddenly having second thoughts about taking this crazy girl to Mount Olympus. I mean, why do I need to take her there anyway? Why does she want to go there in the first place? I know she somehow sent Jason to Mount Olympus, so why don't I just go there myself and pick him up?

I withdraw my outstretched hand.

"What are you doing?" Amelia now has her palm extended upwards. "Didn't you say I have to hold out my hand?"

"How did you know I could take you to Mount Olympus? And why do you want to go there anyway?"

She drops her hand. "I've overheard you and Shana talking a lot."

Why am I not surprised she's an eavesdropper?

"And as for my reasons of going to Mount Olympus, well, let's just say that as a goddess I totally belong there."

"But I thought you said you and Jason would make a the perfect High School couple. How are you going to be a goddess on Mount Olympus *and* be at school at the same time?"

"Well, Jason and I wouldn't be at school all the time. When we hook up we're probably going to get married on Mount Olympus anyway..."

Okay. It's official. This girl is totally bonkers. There's no way I'm going to let her set foot onto the floating island of Mount Olympus. Also, Shana and I had both realized —when she'd disappeared at the dance in a puff of smoke— that this girl is a total drama queen.

"Screw it, you're a wacko." I wave Amelia off and straighten my turban. With a scrunched up face I concentrate on thoughts of limboland. It's a place between the Underworld and Mount Olympus and I'm so busy thinking about the skyward location and its bright puffy-clouded countenance during the day, I fail to see the reason why I haven't yet teleported.

I've never seen limboland at night. I have no idea what it's like to stand atop a cloud in the night sky.

Well, here's hoping I've developed a good enough imagination over time. I haven't exactly seen any sci-fi movies I've ever liked, and I definitely don't watch astronomy documentaries on TV. Instead, I look up at the night sky that hovers above and all around me at this very moment.

"What are you doing?" Amelia sounds concerned.

"I'm going Mount Olympus."

"Don't you mean *we're* going to Mount Olympus?"

"Nope," I say, my gaze still directed upwards. "I'm not taking your loony butt with me."

"Wait. What?" Amelia steps forward. "What do you mean you're not taking me with you? This is why I cursed you in the first place! Do you want to have snake hair forever—"

And that's the last thing I clearly hear from insane Amelia, because my thoughts spring true, lifting me physically towards another land. Although, I think I do hear her shouts of anger drifting on the dark wind.

"You'll never find Jason!"

*

After being whisked through cool air for the briefest of moments, I land on my front atop a dark cloud. I can actually feel the soft folds of the cloud's puffiness as substantial mist. It's like cotton-candy, but only if that treat were made of softest silk from the gods.

I sit up to find my turban is askew, but at least the thing is still intact atop my head. I straighten it and as I'm feeling along the edge I notice a creepy snake has escaped the fabric of my head-wrap. After tucking the straight standing serpent back in, I wipe my fingers on my t-shirt.

Gosh but snake scales feel creepy.

When I get to my feet I discover I hadn't wiped my finger on my t-shirt at all, because that's just not possible considering the fact that I'm now dressed as a Grecian goddess.

I forgot about this. Every time I end up somewhere like limboland, my clothes magically change. I've often wondered how this happens. Does the air in limboland hold within it a magical fashion spell?

Standing up, I dust off bits of cloud from my white silky toga-like dress. I'd feel as though I were wearing a sheet if it weren't for the fact that this gown is elaborately trimmed with exquisite golden ropes and silky braids. Normally, if I were here under normal circumstances, my hair would be transformed into fancy curls right now, but as it stands, I'm stuck with snake-hair.

In the distance I can see the floating island of Mount Olympus. It looks amazing hanging there under the starry night sky. There are lights on the upper surface of the isle that twinkle brightest near the most populated areas.

Now comes the tricky part. In order to get to Mount Olympus, I'm going to have to fly there. I've been on this journey with Jason many times, but he's always been the one to guide us both through the skies. At the moment it's night time, it's very dark and most importantly I don't even know if I'm capable of magically flying by myself.

Here goes nothing!

Pushing off the cloud with my sandal-clad feet, I spring into the air.

This does the trick. I'm airborne and sailing toward Mount Olympus. Dark clouds streak by me below. When I near the floating island the landscape beneath me changes. From way up here I can no longer tell Mount Olympus is hovering in the air. I'm just a regular flying goddess-girl who's cruising through the air over solid land.

"Woooooooo." I howl into the night sky. I could get used to this flying thing. I'm not going fast enough so that my make-shift turban flies off, but neither am I jetting through the clouds too slowly. I'm making good time and I should be able to land in the great Olympian city of Zeus soon.

Landing.

Uh oh. I think this is going to be problematic.

Hhmmmmmm. Maybe if I think about slow moving things, that will help. I picture snails and turtles in my mind and it works! I get my feet under me and land on the stone streets of the ancient Greek styled city within minutes. Actually, the place looks more like an ancient Roman city with its balustrades and soaring columns, but who am I to tell the difference? I never paid attention to ancient studies last year, and now that I'm part of this world it's right in front of my face. I'm immersed in this magical culture. And what an environment it is!

There must be a celebration going on, because throngs of people line the streets. Minor gods and goddesses all dressed in gowns and flowing robes. Creatures large and small roam freely in and out of grand buildings.

Suddenly, I don't feel so out of place. No one around me cares that I'm wearing a toga, or even that I've got a bright pink cloth wrapped around my head.

I don't stand out and that's just how I like it.

Hurrying towards Zeus' palace I make my way inside through an impossibly high archway. It's so bright in this vast complex I feel like I've stepped into daylight. I pass through a massive indoor courtyard with a glass ceiling higher than the entrance archway. It's like an indoor city. This complex is dizzying in its vastness and if I hadn't been here before with Jason, I'd be lost by now.

As I turn around a corner column that rises high into the air, I reach the main pavilion. There are huge seats taking up one half of the circular shaped mezzanine. The seats are stone steps that reach back and upwards like bleachers. It's full of toga-dressed gods and goddesses, while I notice Zeus below on his raised dais. He's addressing the masses, which is good, because he won't notice me sneak by.

After hurrying down wide corridors supported by yet more enormous columns, I find my way to Jason's Olympian quarters.

"Jason?" I call out after opening one of two thick carved wooden doors. I shut it behind me and continue to call out Jason's name. I'm in his bedroom but the place is like a studio apartment for royals. There's even a column platform with Jason's bust, carved from exquisite marble sitting on top. There are historical paintings along the fabric draped walls and the huge crystalline double doors in front of me lead out onto a stone balcony. Outside I can see glittering lights in the night darkened city below.

"Jason? Are you here?" I'm getting desperate now. What if he's not here? What if Amelia was lying to me about where she made him disappear to? Remembering back, I think I heard her utter something about not being able to find Jason on my own.

If that *is* what she said, then I'm screwed. This palace and the entirety of Mount Olympus is massive beyond comprehension. Even though I can view the whole of this floating island from limboland, doesn't mean it's small once you're actually on the island itself.

As if to remind myself of this land's vastness, I move toward the balcony doors. My hand touches onto the golden handle that's enriched with swirls and patterns of leaves. I turn the handle and open the sparkling crystal door.

"Jason?" I step out onto the stone veranda. "Are you — *argh*!" I scream and scream when I see him. Jason is here all right, but it's not the Jason I wanted to see at all.

Floating before me is his ghost.

Jason —my godly boyfriend— is dead!

This can't be happening! Jason and I have only been dating for a matter of weeks! Life is so unfair in the world of gods and goddesses! Why does he have to be dead already? We were so happy! Wait...

Can a god actually die?

Finally, I stop screaming long enough to notice that the ethereal image of my floating boyfriend is waving at me. He's doing something funny with his mouth too.

"Are you trying to say something?" I question him and find my voice is shaky with fear. "Oh my word! You can't talk?"

Ghost Jason shakes his head, confirming my suspicions.

"How did this happen? How did Amelia kill you? I thought gods couldn't die!" I'm hysterical when ghost Jason smacks me across the face. He's transparent though, so of course his hand goes right through my cheek and comes out my left ear.

I gasp in surprise and raise my hand to my cheek as though I've actually been wounded. "You actually tried to slap me?"

Ghost Jason shakes his head as though to say *no*. He gestures at the air with crazy hand movements.

"Oh you knew your smack wouldn't touch me?" I question dubiously. "Well, you're just lucky you're dead because if you had really slapped me I'd kill you."

Ghost Jason smiles.

"You're not actually dead, are you?"

He shakes his head again and relief floods through me. "So what happened? Why are you like a ghost? Why didn't you come to me when I called your name? Why can't you speak?" I'm getting hysterical with questions again and Ghost Jason steps forward. My questions are halted when he puts his hand through mine. "That's so weird." I gasp.

He mouths something to me that I attempt to verbally decipher. "Some... wisp... pee?"

No, no. That's not right. We both shake our heads simultaneously and he tries again.

"Who... wants... free... buttsweep?" I try, but it still doesn't make any sense. "Oh!" I exclaim. "This is pointless! I'm terrible at reading lips!"

Instead of trying again with the lip-reading. Jason floats through the balcony door. He beckons me to follow. Once we reach the wooden doors he passes right through, but obviously I have to open one of them.

When I emerge into the large corridor, from his bedroom, he beckons me further. I follow as Ghost Jason drifts ahead of me. He's wearing godly red robes that reach his knees. Even in translucent form he's dressed-up like a gladiator. Even though it's see-through, the breastplate he's wearing shines with a golden hue. His gladiator sandals reach up high on his calves, where as my own sandals are thankfully ankle length.

"Where are we going?" I huff and puff, running behind Ghost Jason. He doesn't stop and turn to me though, he just floats ahead faster and faster. "Slow down." I complain as we round a column into another corridor. "I've got a stomach cramp!"

Finally, Ghost Jason slows and eventually comes to a stop in front of a small door that's set into the wall. We've come very deep into the palace and the corridor we're in is quite narrow. There's one glowing sconce on the wall. It's a torch light, but the fiery light atop it doesn't burn so much as magically glow with brightness.

Ghost Jason points at the door.

"You want me to go in there?"

He nods and his form continues to bob up and down, his feet never touching the floor. Well, I guess if he were to lower his feet would just go right *through* the floor anyway.

Placing my hand onto the plain brass knob of the door, I try it out. "It's locked."

Ghost Jason flicks his fist twice to the right, once left, then twice right again.

"Oh I get it!" I'm enthusiastic now. "That's like some kind of secret door opening trigger, right?"

I try it.

I turn the knob twice right, once left, then twice right again like a locker combination. Sort of.

"It worked!" I exclaim.

The door creaks open inwardly and Ghost Jason floats past me and inside. His ethereal form vanishes into the darkness beyond the threshold.

"Jason?" I whisper. There's no reply.

Stepping forward with one sandaled foot, I walk through the

doorway and on into the gloom. "Umm... it's really dark in here. Could someone turn on a light?"

Still no answer. Well, Ghost Jason won't be answering me, he can't even talk! I don't know who I think I'm speaking to anyway, really I'm just trying to act like I'm capable of normal conversation. I'm trying to bolster my spirits. It's creepy going in here and my spoken voice still sounds shaky.

"Ouch!" I exclaim as my toe hits something in the dark. "This is stupid. I can't see anything. I'll be right back." After rubbing my sore toe for a few seconds, I turn to move back towards the small open door. The only light coming in from the corridor is on the wall sconce outside. If it's a detachable torch I can remove the thing and bring the light in here. I don't know why I didn't think of this before, I guess I just assumed there would be a magical light in here somewhere.

Bang!

"Oh no!" My eyes go wide in the sudden darkness. The small door has just shut of its own accord. "I can't see! I can't see! Jason, help me!"

I'm rooted to the spot with fear, but there's probably no point in me crying out for Ghost Jason. For all I know he could be standing right next to me. He can't communicate with me physically or verbally though, so if I continue to scream and scream I'm just going to freak out again.

Oh I hate this. I hate darkness so extreme that I can't even see my own hand in front of my face. I know it's immature, but even at home at night I leave the hallway light on and my bedroom door slightly ajar. I can't sleep in pitch darkness! I'm a regular old scaredy-cat!

The darkness is stifling in here! I need to get out! But what if I move in the wrong direction and never find the door?

Well, I've got to at least try. It's so dark in here, not only can I not see, but there's nothing to hear either. It's like existing in a void.

I slide my foot slowly along the floor, pushing it out in front of me. I don't think I turned around in my hysteria, once the door had slammed shut, so if I just keep moving straight ahead I might actually find the door.

Creeping forward one sliding footstep at a time, eventually my previously bonked toe comes into contact with the wall. At least, I hope it's a wall.

Pushing my splayed fingers out in front of me they do indeed make contact with a wall. I feel along the surface. "Yes!" I cry out when my hand finds the doorknob. I wrench and pull at it, but of course it's locked.

"Oh! Duh!" I have to put in the secret knob-turn.

Click twice left.. twice right... No. Wait. That's not right!

"Calm down, Kate. You can do this." I envision the outer corridor. Turn right twice... once left... twice right again and hey presto!

Nothing.

The stupid door is still locked.

"No! No! No!" I pound my fist onto the door in frustration then lean my forehead insufferably onto it. With my hands I feel all along the door frame. "What the heck...?"

My fingers touch onto a knobbly, protruding object that I flick upwards.

"My eyes!" I'm suddenly blinded by light. Wonderful, amazing light that I momentarily can't see anything through.

Blinking rapidly I turn around as my eyes adjust. When the

haziness depletes, objects come into focus and I find myself staring at the most unusual thing any god or goddess of Mount Olympus could ever hope to see on this side of limboland.

A drum set.

I'm looking at a glittering gold trimmed set of stage drums, the likes of which have probably been used by the most glamorous of nineteen eighties glam rock band members.

Okay so there *are* other things in this open space too. A space that's relatively small in comparison to the rest of the vast palace I've just been racing through.

Besides the drum set and other rock star equipment —standing microphone, guitar and amplifier— there are many, many green marble statues in here. In fact, there's one statue directly in front of me and I figure it must be the one I'd stubbed my toe on in the dark.

Oh that abysmal darkness, who knew it would be overcome with a simple flick of a switch. That's right. The knobbly thing I'd flicked with my finger turned out to be a light-switch. It's embedded in the wall right next to the small door, a door that from this side is as ordinary as the wall in which its framed.

The walls of this place consist of wooden shelves that are weighed down by yet more green statues. Statues of strange creatures that I couldn't begin to name, but resemble the living creatures I've often seen scampering around on Mount Olympus. Statues of normal creatures like bunnies and squirrels. On the floor of this room are the human shaped statues, all in various repose of what can only be described as pure agony.

As a matter of fact, the green statue I'd stubbed my toe on is that of a man. His body is twisted at the waist and his frozen stone features show an open mouth in the shape of a terrorized scream. I creep forward and look down into the throat of the man statue. It actually goes way down and I think that if I were to shine a light in there I'd be able to see down to its sculptured stomach.

"Weird." I mumble. "It's as though there's a real person frozen in there."

"You've almost got it right."

"Argh!" I scream, startled beyond belief. I turn around so fast my skirts twirl and swish around my legs. After jumping behind the green man statue, I dare to peek around the side. "Who the crud are you...? You scared me to death!"

There's a guy standing in the very spot I just vacated. He's got his hands tucked into black jeans, his hair is long to his shoulders and it's so black it shines blue. He's wearing a black skull t-shirt and blackest of all are his eyes. *All* of his eyes are black. He doesn't have any whites in his eyeballs and it's majorly creepy.

"That's a first." He raises an eyebrow. "I don't think I've ever been asked what kind of crud I am."

"I didn't mean... I just said crud because..." Oh screw this. Why am I apologising? He's the one who jumped out at me. "What's wrong with your eyes?"

"Thaddeus Marcus Magnus Helios of Thebes."

"What?"

"That's who the crud I am, but you can call me Thad." He smiles and the whiteness of his teeth seems to glare in sharp contrast to his dark countenance. "And as for my eyes... well... let's just say they work much better this way. Besides, I could ask you what's up with your turban."

I don't know what his cryptic answer is supposed to mean, and his answer with a question about my pink head-wrap might just be his way of trying to further confuse me. "Well what do want?"

"What do *I* want? You're the stranger here." He leans against a nearby statue of a frozen woman whose head is bowed as though in despair. "What do you want? I don't think I've ever had a visit from a goddess before, and I've been here for quite some time."

I can't quite place his accent. This guy, Thaddeus Whateverus, has very unnerving black eyes, yet somehow he doesn't make me feel fearful. His clothes are modern and of the mortal world, but his words seem ancient now and then.

"Ehem." I clear my throat nervously and step out from behind the green statue. I figure if the guy was going to attack me he could have done so without introducing himself first. "I'm Kate. Just Kate. I'm not a goddess."

"You must be a demi-goddess then, or you wouldn't be here now. Well, you wouldn't be here as you are."

I wouldn't? "Why not?"

"Because mortals can't exist in here as anything but stone." He removes a hand from his pocket and raps his knuckles against the statue of a depressed looking goddess.

"What are you saying?" My eyes bulge and I look around. "Are these statues of people turned to stone?" I suddenly feel really weirded out by the statue of the screaming man I was hiding behind, so I move quickly away. "What is this place?" I glance up at the ceiling feeling lost.

"This is the garage of lost stone."

The what now? Tilting my head back down, I peer into his black eyes. "Your answers rarely make sense. Are we really communicating on the same level here? Thad, was it?"

He lowers his gaze and stuffs his hand back into his pocket. "I can answer you that easily, I said you could call me Thad. As for your other query. I can only apologise, Kate, was it?"

Does he mock me, I wonder? I nod, and he continues.

"Considering the fact that I've had to learn over one hundred modern languages in the past two years, I think I've done quite well."

I think this guy really has a story to tell and it's very distracting. "I'd love to hear all about your language learning, but I've got a serious problem on my hands, Thad."

"Oh? And what problem would that be?"

"I've totally lost my dead boyfriend somewhere in here. I mean... I don't think he's actually dead, but he is a ghost. He floated in here just before I did, but then he disappeared completely and I haven't seen him since."

"Your ghost boyfriend, huh?" Thad removes his pocketed hand once again so he can scratch his chin. "Does your dead boyfriend have a name?"

"Yeah, Jason—"

"Me."

Turning, I find the very god I was just speaking of. He's just appeared through the door! "Jason!" I shout and run to him. I seem to have forgotten about his intangible countenance though, so as I move to hug him, I run straight through his form.

I'm empty handed with palms up and the ghost of my boyfriend is behind me. I turn around to find him panting.

"I knew it!" I exclaim. "You're not dead because ghosts can't get out of breath! Why are you breathing hard anyway? Have you been running? Oh my gosh you spoke!"

I clamp my lips shut before more crazy blatherings of hysteria can escape my mouth in verbal form. My boyfriend ghost said one simple word, while I just shouted about one-hundred of them.

"Is she always like this?" Thad jerks a thumb in my direction.

"I take offense to that!" I pause, pondering what he's insinuating. "What am I supposedly *like* anyway?"

"A chatterbox. My chatterbox." My floating ghost of a boyfriend smiles and my whole world lights up. He called me his *my*! He's so sweet, even in less than substantial form.

"You can be a chatterbox too now, I see." My eyebrows raise expectantly. "You can talk and I can totally hear you."

"Yes, I can. And I have a lot of questions for you." Jason asks me about how he ended up here when all he remembers was being at the dance. I tell him and Thad about everything that happened after he disappeared from the school. "But I don't know why you're a ghost."

"It's part of the gorgon curse." Thad says. "If what you're telling us is true, then it sounds like Medusa's daughter Amelia is messing with powers she can't control."

How does he know all this? "So is she the one who can turn Jason solid again?"

Thad nods.

"And this room is sort of like your limboland, Kate." Jason gestures around. "It's in-between the mortal and godly realms."

"It is?"

Jason Ghost nods his head. "And it's been Thad's home for the past two years."

"You guys know each other?" I look from floating Jason to Thad and back again.

"Of course we do." Thad says. "We're in the same band together...

at least… we used to be."

Okay. This is weird. I've met some of Jason's godly friends on Mount Olympus, but if this place is an in-between, I don't know where we are, what's going on, or who's who."

"How come you were out there just now?" I point at the door.

"I went looking for Thad, but I see you found him." Jason says.

"But you floated in here first when the room was dark, why didn't you help me find that light switch?" I tip my head questioningly at Jason. I'm getting all mixed up in the head and I think some proper explanations are in order. Sighing loudly, I sit down onto a statue that's shaped like a bench. Okay so really it's the statue of a man on all fours, and I'm now sitting on his back, but it's a flat (ish) surface, so it will have to do. "Would either of you care to explain?" I start ticking off questions on my fingers.

"A… what are we doing here? B… who are you really?" I glare at Thad, but look away when he returns that black stare. "C… are you going to remain a ghost forever?" My gaze turns sympathetic towards my hovering boyfriend. "And D… how come you're dressed normal?"

My eyes wander back toward Thad. His eyebrows raise in curiosity that in no way detracts from the deep dark pools of his eyes.

"Would you like to go first?" Ghost Jason intones, looking at Thad.

"No, no. You go ahead."

"Okay, Kate." Jason floats closer to me. "Thaddeus here was a warrior of Thebes who was taken from his home land thousands of years ago and renamed thusly. He was unfortunate enough to come across Medusa when she was eighteen years of age, just like him.

She stared at him, he turned to stone on the spot and then *blam!* Two thousand years later he wakes up here. Medusa's snake head was returned to normal and she had gathered the remnants of statues she'd created over time. Since marrying a Titan and settling in your town, Kate. Medusa has been finding ways to undo the stone curse on each of these mortals, as well as upon creatures. Every stone curse is personal to the individual. Like that dude you're sitting on."

At this point, I stand up and get off the poor man's back. He might be made of stone, but now that I know he's a real person, I feel guilty as hell about perching my butt on his back side. I don't interrupt Jason though.

"Thad was released from Medusa's stone curse." My boyfriend continues. "But his circumstances were different and he can't leave this room. He can only travel as far as my rooms within the castle." Jason turns to Thad. "Your turn."

"Sure thing." Thad bows low and I notice a dark tendril of hair falls over his forehead. He extends his arm when he stands. "Right this way, if you please."

I follow him behind my floating see-through boyfriend. When Thad pushes his hair back with his fingers, I'm reminded of the moment when I had to tuck a stray snake back under my turban.

I shudder at the memory.

I hope all of this ancient history information is leading somewhere, because right now I really want to find out how any of this new knowledge is going to help Jason's ghostly predicament.

"So he's like two-thousand-twenty years old?" I whisper to Jason.

"He doesn't remember the years while he was a stone statue, Kate. And anyway, how did you know he was awakened for two years in this room?"

"You said this place has been his home for two years, ever since he awoke from his statue sleep. I did the math."

"Oh."

We weave our way around statues in various forms of repose. Most faces of the green statues look frozen in abject terror, but some look as though they welcomed their stone fate, just before it happened.

When we emerge from the maze of statues I'm utterly astonished at the open space we enter.

We're in a garage. A garage that's been decorated to look like a living-room. There are throw rugs on the concrete floor. On top of the rugs are couches. There's a desk with a computer on it and another desk holds a forty inch TV.

"We are totally in a garage." I say flatly. I remember Thad saying something about a garage. "The garage of lost stone is literally a garage?"

"Yeah, we used to practice in here." Thad moves to the left of the double-wide garage door and presses a button on the wall. It opens by rolling upward. When the aluminum door is finally fully open, I find myself looking out onto a street of normality.

"Wow. You weren't kidding when you said this place was in-between." It really is a suburban street out there. I can see houses lined on the opposite side of the road. "So back through the statues and that door is Zeus' palace on Mount Olympus, and through this garage opening is… is…" What is it I'm seeing here?

"Holy cow!" I yell excitedly in amazement as recognition kicks in. "That's a street in our town. That's Shana's street, isn't it?"

Jason nods his partially transparent head in answer, and Thad nods his solid noggin too.

"Well that's terrific! Let's get out of here so we can go home and find stupid Amelia! I'm tired of having snakes for hair and she needs to turn you back into a solid person!" I've figured by now that it must have been an added bonus curse that Amelia put upon my boyfriend, when she'd caused him to disappear at the school dance. She's the idiot who's responsible for everything that's wrong in our lives at the moment, and she's going to be the one to put things right, even if I have to strangle the girl with my bare hands.

I don't care how this garage got here. I don't need to know why it looks out the same street my best friend Shana lives on. I'm just glad to be near my home.

With a renewed sense of perseverance I move toward the open garage door.

"No, Kate!"

But Jason's warning is too late. I hit some kind of invisible wall that blocks me from escaping the confines of the garage. Not only that, whatever magical field it was that blocks my way also blows me backwards and I land with a *fwump* onto a (thankfully) overstuffed sofa.

The turban has been blasted off my head. The snakes are writhing, snapping, biting my cheeks. One slithery serpent attacks my eye and it's at this point that I cry out in fear.

"Thad, help her!" Jason cries.

The next thing I know there's a warm pressure on the back of my waist. "Up we go." Thad whisks me up off the couch. "Now hold still," he says, pressing his free hand to my forehead.

Warmth from his hand seeps into my cranium and the snakes go still and hang limply from my scalp.

"How did you do that?" I ask him, gazing into his black eyes as he takes his hand away from my forehead.

His only response is to wink one of those dark eyes. The warmth of his hand is now also removed from my back as he steps away towards the garage door.

"He doesn't like to talk about his powers." Ghost Jason whispers to me when he floats closer. "It has to do with his curse." He points with two fingers at his eyes. "Are you all right? We'll get your snake hair fixed now. I'm curious though. What does it actually feel like having snakes attached to your head?"

"It's gross." I'm feeling really self-conscious about my serpent hair, so I scramble to grab the pink fabric off the sofa. After wrapping it tightly —yet admittedly sloppily— around my hair-snakes, I look up at floating Jason. "Can you really fix my hair and get it back to normal?"

"Well I can't, but Amelia can. And now that you're here, you and Thad can take us from this place."

I think I know what my see-through boyfriend is talking about. Like Thad, I too am part of a world in-between. "What do I have to do to get us out of here?" Do we need to go back to limboland?"

"Yes, but not that way, Thad can't travel through Zeus' palace. And the only way to your limboland is by flying, so…"

"Yeah," I frown deeply. "I know. But why do we need him with us anyway?"

"I'll show you why." Ghost Jason floats close to Thad and grabs his arm.

"You're touching him!" I exclaim. "Your hand isn't going through him."

"Just another benefit of my curse." Thad looks bemused and I remember how Jason said he doesn't like talking about his curse, so I'm definitely not going to ask him anything.

"I knew Thad was the one who could help us, Kate. Now take his hand so we can walk out of here for real this time."

I'm a little worried about whatever invisible wall is blocking the garage entrance, but I trust Jason wouldn't let me get blasted off my feet again. So I do take Thad's hand in mine and together we all step forward. Well, Thad and I walk and Jason floats.

"You can open your eyes, Kate." Jason's voice is reassuring. I listen to his words and lift my lids.

We're outside on Shana's street and it's night time. "We made it." I mumble gratefully.

"This is incredible." Thad releases my hand and walks to the curb. Once there he looks to the left and then the right.

"What's he doing?" I ask Jason.

"This is his first time in the mortal realm."

I look at Jason, shocked. "It is? But he took us safely past that invisible garage wall."

"Only because you're here, Kate. Your powers of the in-between of limboland combined with his has set him free."

"You mean Thad was trapped as a statue for thousands of years, and then trapped in that garage for two years?"

Jason Ghost nods his transparent head. "At least he's free from the confines of that garage now, even if he'll never be free of his curse."

Thad's mysterious curse. We should probably find a way to help the guy, but first I think there are a couple of urgent problems that need fixing. The first one being that my boyfriend is a frikin ghost! My snake-hair-problem actually comes second on my list of important matters, because even though I've got scaly squirmy hair, at least my body is solid.

"I spoke with Thad when I first appeared on Mount Olympus as a ghost. We didn't know what was happening." Jason is trying to explain things too me, but all I can seem to think about is getting to Amelia so we can do away with our own stupid curses.

I don't interrupt Jason though, and he continues.

"Thad and I both thought it best, at the time, if we didn't tell Zeus. I was waiting for you, Kate. I knew you would find me."

"You're damn right I did! And thanks for not telling your dad!" I'm guessing Jason realized what the repercussions of Zeus finding out about this fiasco would be. He'd probably blast straight down here on a bolt of lightning, sending all the Titans back to Tartarus in a flash.

"Thank you, Kate." Thad has rejoined us. "It's nice to be able to see what's beyond the houses on the other side of the street. Those buildings," he turns and points a finger at the houses opposite. "They're the only buildings I've seen outside that garage door for the past two years. It's a very boring view compared to the modern societies I've seen on TV and the internet." He winks a glittering black eye.

"So." Jason Ghost interjects. "Should we all go see our dear friend, Amelia?"

If he were solid he'd get a punch in the arm for such a remark. "Don't even joke about that girl being a friend." I hiss.

"You're right. He should be calling me his girlfriend."

Collectively, all three of us look up just as Amelia steps from the bushes.

"So you actually found him." Amelia looks Jason up and down.

"Although, you didn't exactly find him in the best of forms, now did you, Kate?" Amelia throws her head back and laughs. Actually, she cackles like a witch. And what's with her outfit?

"What are you wearing?" I glare at her.

"This?" She twirls around. "It's one of my mother's Grecian frocks. I think it goes well with my new status as a goddess. It's better than what you're wearing."

Taking immediate offense, I pat down my pink turban to make sure it's secure. When we had stepped out of the statue garage my goddess robes had returned to a normal t-shirt and jeans. Even Jason as a ghost is now dressed for modern mortal times, albeit transparent jeans and t-shirt.

"Change him back to normal." I'm surprised to hear my voice sounds so calm. My insides are twisting with anger at Amelia, just like the snakes on my head would be twisting and turning if it hadn't been for Thad stepping in.

"You're blaming his death on me? And who's this freak?" She juts her chin at Thad. "His eyes are disgusting."

Blam!

I punch Amelia in the face and she goes down.

Wow that felt good. No wonder Shana wasn't able to control herself when she'd hit Amelia at the dance. It's really nice punching someone who deserves it.

"You bitch!" Amelia spits a glob of blood onto the side-walk. Under the light of the street-lamps it looks like a spray of black. "I'm never going to undo the gorgon curse." She scrapes up onto her feet, but stumbles on the long flowing fabric of her blue velvet dress. "You're going to have snake hair for the rest of your life!"

Amelia turns to leave, but Jason yells for her to return. At least, I think that's what he's trying to do, but no words escape his lips.

"I was afraid this might happen." Thad runs a worried hand through his long dark hair.

Jason is floating after the rapidly departing Amelia. When he zooms in front of her, she stops walking. Thad and I catch up to them. Jason Ghost touches Thad's shoulder and mouths words to him.

"I understand," he says, when Jason is done.

"You heard him?" My eyes are wide with concern. "What did he say?"

"He said he's going to date Amelia."

Now my eyes are on the verge of bugging out of my head in shock. "He what?" I blurt.

Thad sighs loudly. "Amelia," he says, still looking at the ground. "If you'll free Kate from the gorgon curse, Jason has promised he'll become your boyfriend. And I can vouch for him, because I'm the one who can make him solid again.

What's happening here? Jason doesn't look convinced and I notice Thad steps away when he tries to touch his shoulder again. Is there something else Jason wants to say? And does he really think I'm going to let him date Amelia in exchange for getting rid of the snakes on my head? "What's going to stop her from cursing me with snake-hair again anyway? This is a crazy idea and I won't do it!"

"You don't have a choice." Thad grabs my hand and locks onto Jason's arm at the same time.

Suddenly, Jason grabs my free hand and it doesn't go straight through!

"What are you doing?" Amelia shrieks. "I... I can't move!" She's locked in the middle of our small circle that's linked by holding hands.

I don't know what's going on and I'm about to question Thad when I notice an incredible change within his black eyes. There's something in there. Something that I can't escape. I'm lost in his dark gaze as a powerful wind kicks up all around us.

Someone screams.

Snakes pour out of Thad's eye sockets.

The pink cloth is ripped from my head. I can feel the snakes come to life as they writhe and twist, stretching to be freed from my scalp.

And still I stare into Thad's eyes that ooze serpent after serpent.

I can feel the slithering creatures sliding up my legs and soon enough I'm covered and consumed completely by hissing snakes.

"Ack! Ack! Snakes! Get them off me!"

My arms are pinned under the weight of what must be a giant boa constrictor.

"Kate! Chill out!"

"Shana?"

Blinking my eyes open I see that my query was right. It *is* Shana who's hovering over me now. "What happened?" Sitting up, I rub my forehead in confusion. There are no snakes anywhere and I seem to be sitting safely on a sofa in Shana's house. I push my fingers further upwards and when they touch hair, I scream.

"My hair! I have hair!"

"About time you woke up!" Jason runs to me and Shana moves aside. He grapples me into a hug and then kisses me on the lips.

"You're solid!" I screech. "You're not a ghost and I have hair! I have hair, Jason, not snakes!" Pinging out a strand of my dark hair, I yank it hard, just to make sure I'm not dreaming all of this. "Ouch." When I know the pulling of hair actually hurts, it's confirmed. This is for real. "But how did I end up in here?"

"I saw you guys out there," Shana says. "Wow! What a show!"

"I thought you were covering for me at my parents." I look at her. She's sitting in an armchair and Jason moves aside.

"I am, you've only been gone like thirty minutes and we should be able to make it back to your house totally unscathed."

Thirty minutes? "You're crazy, I've been gone way longer than that. I went to Mount Olympus and everything."

"Remember, Kate. Time passes differently on Mount Olympus. "Jason smiles at me.

"I guess." I harrumph loudly. "It's getting to the point where every time I visit there, less and less time passes here." I wonder what's up with that. I also wonder what the heck happened to Amelia and Thad.

As though reading my thoughts through my bulging eye expression, Jason cuts in. "Amelia went home. I think she saw reason about the fact that I'm never going to date her. And it's all thanks to that guy." He points behind the sofa we're sitting on and I turn around.

Standing in the open walk-way is Thad. As usual, he's got his hands stuffed into the pockets of his black jeans, and he's leaning against the wall-frame. "Just returning the favor."

I turn my head to look at Shana. She shrugs her shoulders as though she doesn't have a clue about what's going on.

"Thad took Amelia's powers." Jason says.

I turn back around to face Thad. "You can do that?" I ask him.

He nods, but doesn't further elaborate.

"Both of her curses were undone, Kate." Jason smiles when I look at him. "No more snake hair for you and no more ghostly floating around for me."

I return his smile, but I also share it with Thad. "Thank you," is all I say. I've already learned that he's a very private guy. Not willing to share anything really.

"Okay!" Shana jumps to her feet. "If you're feeling better, Kate, we should get back to your parents before they find out you left in the first place." She comes over to me and pulls me off the couch. "And you can tell me *everything* that happened on Mount Olympus. And I mean *everything.*" She whispers when we're out of earshot of Jason and Thad.

We all leave Shana's house through the back yard.

"I'll see you tomorrow at eight in the morning, sharp." Jason blows me a kiss.

Shana makes retching noises. "You two love-birds make me want to throw up some times. And don't you dare show up at Kate's at eight in the morning. Don't you know a girl needs mega amounts of beauty sleep after being inflicted with snake hair?"

Jason looks at me for an answer. All I can do is shrug my shoulders. "Apparently she's the one who's in charge of my sleeping hours now." I point at Shana briefly.

"Fine... I'll umm... I'll see you, Shana and Thad tomorrow afternoon."

I smile and nod and I'm about to turn to leave when something he said gnaws at me. "Wait. What?"

"I'm afraid certain things come at a price, Kate." Jason awkwardly shoves his hands into the pockets of his jeans. "I wasn't one-hundred percent okay with what Thad did, but I didn't have a choice."

"What are you saying?" Shana asks this so I don't have to.

"You'll just be seeing a bit more of me for a while, Kate." Thad steps forward and punches me right in the stomach.

I'm so surprised by his movements it takes a second for it to register — he didn't punch me in the stomach. His hand is sticking straight through my middle!

He pulls it out again and his hand goes straight back into the pocket of his jeans.

"Oh my god! You're a ghost!" Shana whispers loudly so as not to wake the entire neighbourhood.

"How did this happen?" I whisper/shout too. "Was it when you took the ghost curse off Jason? How come you're not see-through like Jason was?" Here I go again, chattering away with questions.

"Oh man." Shana drags a hand down her face. "We don't have time for this, Kate. Your parents!"

Shana's right. I've got so many questions that will have to wait for tomorrow when I see Jason and Thad again—

"Wait," I say to my boyfriend. "Where is Thad going? Did I hear you say you'd see us and him tomorrow?"

"Ehem." Jason nervously clears his throat. "Yeah, I'll see you all tomorrow. Thad can explain things to you on your way back to your parent's."

And with that my newly re-solidified boyfriend walks —no— he *runs* away.

"Coward," Thad mumbles and shakes his head. There's a sneaky scowl on his face right before he vanishes completely.

"Oh!" Shana exclaims. "He really is an invisible ghost!"

I'm shocked. I don't know what's going on. "Let's just go." Taking Shana's arm, I pull her down the night darkened street. I've decided this whole situation is just too much for my traumatised mind to figure out tonight.

*

Aaahhh bed. It's so cosy not having to even think about lying down with snakes for hair. I don't know what I would have done if I'd been inflicted with the gorgon curse for, like, the rest of my life!

But it's all okay now. I don't know why everything is okay, except for the fact that Thad did something tonight that saved Jason and I from undesirable lifestyles. Jason as a ghost and me as a modern Medusa just wouldn't have worked out.

I don't know what it is that Thad did with whatever powers he holds, but I'm eternally grateful to him.

As I snuggle down under my covers I call out a thank you. "Thanks, Thad, wherever you are."

"You're welcome, and I'm right here."

Holy mother of all that is freak-out-city!

I sit up in bed. I'm so out of my mind with shock that when I go to turn on my lamp, I tumble out of bed instead.

"Ouch!" After scrabbling around I find the switch and flick on the light. "Whaa... what are you doing here?" I jump to my feet and there stands Thad, leaning casually against the frame of my bedroom door.

"It's only a temporary problem, Kate. Go back to bed."

"A temporary...? What kind of answer...?" Pausing, I get to grips with my lungs before I hyperventilate from frustration. "I asked you why you're here." Looking up, I'm suddenly aware of the fact that I'm only wearing a t-shirt as pyjamas. Thad's dark eyes, that have no whites at all, are locked onto me, so I jump back into bed and pull the covers up to my chin. "Explain."

"There were some side-effects to the shifting of powers that I performed tonight." Thad grumbles, his gaze is unwavering and for a moment I find myself getting once again lost in the darkness of his eyes.

I blink rapidly and look away as Thad continues. "Until Jason and I can find a solution, I'm afraid my translucent form is connected to you, Kate. Where you go, I go. But again. It's only temporary."

"How do you know that?"

"Know what?"

"Argh!" I huff in exasperation and punch down my blanket. "How do you know that this situation, which requires you to follow me around, is only temporary?"

Thad removes one hand from his pocket, he shakes his finger pointedly. "I'm not exactly following you around by choice. Actually, I don't have a choice in the matter. In order to return Jason to his solid form, and for you to be rid of the gorgon curse, I had to take on Amelia's powers, and also... umm..." He scratches his head. He looks nervous.

"You took on our curses?" I frown deeply. Why would he do that? "But I thought you took Amelia's powers."

Thad shakes his head. "Not exactly. Her powers are held within me, but only as the curses they are. I can't use her powers... not yet anyway."

Now what's that supposed to mean? "You know what?"

"What?"

"I don't care."

"You don't?"

"Nope." I snuggle back down under my blanket. "I'm just glad I don't have snake hair anymore. Wait!" I sit bolt upright again. "You saved me and Jason and now you're, like, cursed a million times over? I changed my mind! I do care! What can we do about this? How can we save you, Thaaaaadd—"

He moves toward me so fast it's like one minute he was standing halfway across the room, and the next thing I know the dude is right in front of my face.

"I think you should get some rest, Kate." His voice is low. Mesmerizing even. In combination with the dark sparkling orbs of his eyes, I'm at a loss for words. When I look into his gaze it's as though I'm staring deep into the night sky. Is that even possible? I don't know. What I do know is that there really are endless dark depths to Thad's eyes. It's like peering into two cavernous telescopes. I can see the universe in his eyes. Stars like pinpoints draw me deeper into his gaze. They are tiny worlds of light within all the darkness that his eyes reveal.

I'm lost and wandering into unconsciousness. My mind knows peace and calm as I drift into the land of dreams. The last thing I hear as my waking moments are depleted, are the words of a stranger.

Thad's voice resonates into my being. "There are consequences, Kate," he whispers. "There are always consequences for the gods."

STORY IV

Rock Star

As we traverse the treacherous terrain of the underground steps, I'm mentally berating myself for ever agreeing to this insane meeting.

"I don't like it down here, Kate. What if there are snakes lurking in hidden corners?"

My best friend Shana sure has a way with words that instantly make a bad situation worse. In my fearful mind anyway.

"Please don't talk about snakes!" I cringe inwardly and carry on down the stone stairs.

"Oh sorry... I forgot."

She forgot? My best friend in all the world forgot that mere weeks ago my whole head was plastered with snakes? "That's the reason we're down here, Shana. If it weren't for that stupid gorgon curse, we wouldn't be meeting with this person in the first place."

When I say person, I mean being. Or do I? What should I term the individual Shana and I are meeting with tonight?

"I can't see!" Shana screeches. "Put the lamp behind you before I trip down these stupid steps. Remind me again why we had to come down here with a whale oil lamp and not regular flashlights?"

"I guess it's just one of those things. You know? Freaky people always demand freaky stuff."

"Oh you know a lot of freaks, do you?"

"Ssshhh." I stop Shana from speaking. "Did you hear that?"

There's a few seconds of silence before Shana starts talking again.

"Hear what?"

"I thought I heard a squishing noise."

"Squishy?"

"Yeah." Creeping forward I take the final step to the bottom of the twisting stairwell. Moving close to the wall, I'm about to turn the corner when I realize Shana isn't behind me. "Get over here, you wuss."

"You go ahead." She says.

I lift the metal and glass lamp I'm holding. The small flame flickers on the wick inside. "If I go you'll be in the dark."

Sighing loudly, Shana finally joins me. "Fine, but you can be the one to find out about that squishing noise."

And I am indeed the one who finds out, because as I turn the corner the squishing sound reveals itself in the form of a giant eyeball. "Argh!" I scream and take a step back.

"What's the matter — argh!" Shana screams too and runs away.

I, however, am rooted to the floor in trepidation. This is the (gulp) individual we've come to meet, so I have to stand my ground because I'm not sure how else I'm supposed to react when face to face with the world's only living Cyclops. A one-eyed individual who is the source of the squishing noises as he rubs and pokes at his one eye, which is right smack in the middle of his face.

"Hi!" I say exuberantly. "I'm k-k-Kate." My shaky voice betrays any attempts at courtesy. "We were told you could help us."

Squish. Rub. Rub. Cyclops continues to rub his one eye with a thick meaty finger that doesn't seem to have a nail on it. He looks like an ogre dressed in rags.

"I'll help you if you help me." Cyclops' voice is unusually high-pitched for one so large. "I've got something in my eye. Can you help me get it out?"

Oh jeez. This is going to be gross. "Umm yeah, sure I can."

Stepping forward I hold my lantern high. Cyclops pulls down his one and only bottom lid. "I think a bug flew in there," he peeps in his rather squeaky voice. "Can you see anything?"

"Oh my gosh!" I screech, leaning ever closer. "What the heck is that?"

Cyclops does have something stuck in his huge eye, and it isn't just a bug. "Shana, you have got to see this!" Pinching the offending object between index finger and thumb I yank an entire bat out of Cyclops' eye.

"Aaahhh." The large being sighs. I think if he were standing he'd be at least eight feet tall. "That's better."

Dropping the squirming bat, it plops onto the stone floor with a *splat*. However, the thing isn't dead. I know this because within a matter of seconds it flaps its wings and flies away.

"Kate?" Shana puts her head around the corner. "Are you alive?"

I don't answer for a few seconds. Cyclops blinks with a grin on his face. I think he just winked at me for my prank on my wimpy best friend.

"Kate!" Shana screams.

"Chill!" I reply. "Of course I'm not dead. I could have been killed though. Thanks for bailing on me."

Shana drags herself into the cavernous room, slowly scraping her way towards me. "S-s-sorry, Kate. I j-j-just don't do well with strangers."

That's a nice way of putting it. Saying *stranger*. I'm sure she'd realistically like to describe Cyclops as a blatant monster.

"Oh!" Shana startles. "Where did the Cyclops go?"

Say what? How can she fail to see the giant person—

"Where did he go?" I cry, after turning around.

"I'm here." That peeping, squeaking voice is coming from behind us now.

Shana jumps and grabs my arm. I nearly drop the lamp I'm holding. "Don't do that!" I howl, trying to shake her off. She won't budge, so I'm forced to walk forward with best friend attached.

When the light spills on the source of the voice I'm surprised to find Cyclops standing at the base of the stone stairs.

He has shrunk. He's normal sized. Wait, no! He's shrinking ever further.

"What's happening to it?" Shana whispers.

She expects *me* to have the answer to her question?

Once Cyclops has shrunk to the size of a mouse, he waves us over. "Pick me up." He orders, reaching his arms up like a toddler yearning for its mother.

I do as instructed. Bending, I scoop the tiny Cyclops into my hand. "How did you do that?"

He shrugs his tiny shoulders and blinks his one eye while making himself comfortable in the palm of my hand. "I don't have a definitive size where mortals are concerned."

Oh well la dee dah. "I'm not 100% mortal." I'll have him know.

"I think he meant me." Shana whimpers. How she can still be afraid of a mouse sized Cyclops is beyond me.

"No, I meant the mortal realm." Cyclops' squeaky voice makes sense in relation to his new found size. "Now, can we please get out of this hovel? I've been sleeping for a thousand years and I could really do with stretching my legs."

Placing the teensy tiny Cyclops into the pocket of my plaid shirt,

I make my way up the winding stone staircase with Shana.

We're going out into the world so that our new little friend can stretch his legs. The question is, how far will he stretch them? I'm hoping once we get to the surface of this underground lair he doesn't grow into a fifty foot monster.

*

Once we do reach the surface we come out into the grotto of an ancient town church. I never knew the catacombs beneath our town even existed until now.

Making our way to the forefront of the church, Shana and I have to sit down in one of the pews to catch our breath.

"I think I need to start going to the gym." She huffs and puffs with exhaustion. "I had no idea my legs were so out of shape!"

I know how she feels. After climbing all those stone stairs my own legs feel like jello.

Nevertheless, I hoik myself up and we head outside. Once on the surrounding graveyard lawn, I take Cyclops carefully out of my pocket and place him onto the grass.

"What are you doing?" He shouts up at me.

"I'm letting you stretch your legs." I assume this is where he'll grow back to his humongous size.

"Oh right. Yes of course."

Shana and I watch as the miniature Cyclops grows only his legs to five feet in length. They shrink down again and nothing else happens.

"Is that it?" Shana comments.

"Yes." Cyclops puts his arms up and waves inwardly. "Now put me back into your pocket. It's the only way to navigate with my eye."

I look at Shana. She returns my curious gaze.

Picking up Cyclops I put him back into the pocket of my checkered blouse.

Shana looks curiously at tiny Cyclops. "So does this mean your eye works like a magical Satellite Navigation device?"

Cyclops leans on the fold of my pocket, rubbing his receding chin inquisitively. "From what my eye has glanced of mortals over the years, I'd say yes. My eye is like a SatNav. Although... my eye actually works."

"Why?" Shana inquires. "Because your eye is magic?"

"Precisely." Cyclops replies. "You mortals and your technology. You really are tapping into the universe all wrong."

"But we've got scientists." I'm feeling a bit defensive of my mortal heritage.

"Science is a discipline of mortals and it doesn't approach the elements properly."

Rolling my two eyes, I put out the fire in the oil lamp. "Whatever. I think technology is cool."

"Not when your computer crashes." Shana interjects.

I can feel Cyclops nodding in agreement with her. I don't need to look at my pocket to confirm his insolent movements. I don't know why I'm so defensive of mortal technology. I guess it's because all of this powerful magical stuff is new to me. Shana, of all people, should be equally as impressed.

Oh well. Now isn't the time for arguing. We found Cyclops for a reason, and that reason needs to be dealt with asap.

"So you know why we searched you out, right?" I look down at Cyclops in my pocket. It's giving me a crick in my neck, but I can't complain. *We* need *his* help.

He nods. "The Fates informed me of your plight without alerting

Zeus."

Phew. That's a relief. I have to watch my back at every turn to make sure Zeus doesn't know about anything that's happening. We're always on the verge of discovery in this town. It's because of the fact that most of the residents here are on permitted leave from Tartarus by Zeus himself. If Zeus finds out about any problems caused, my dad —and any other Titans living in this town— will be cast back into Tartarus; a realm beneath even that of the Underworld.

"If we're going to find your boyfriend Thad I'll need you to take me to the place where it happened."

I'm already on the move with Shana, who giggles. "He's not my boyfriend!" I shout. "I'm dating Jason, not stupid Thad."

"All right. Calm down." Cyclops' squeaky voice isn't very authoritative. I'm indebted to him though, so I had better calm down indeed.

A few minutes later we've arrived at the precise location where *it* happened. The disaster caused by Thad.

We are at Lakepoint high school.

"Tell me everything that occurred." Cyclops blinks and it looks so weird from my vantage point above his tiny head.

"Well!" Shana takes the oil lamp from me and sets it onto a low brick wall. "Thad's ego grew massive and he kidnapped the whole town to be his groupies! I mean, who does that?" She throws her hands up into the air, exasperated.

I look down at Cyclops. He returns my gaze with his all-seeing one eye. "Like I said. Please tell me everything that occurred."

Scratch that. His *selective* all-seeing eye. He can only help in his own way.

All three of us sit onto the low wall. Well, myself and Shana sit. Cyclops just keeps standing inside my pocket while resting his arms on the flap, causing it to fold a bit.

I start talking...

"Last night the town was gathered for the annual high school talent show. Jason's band was playing so of course I was going to be there. Me and Shana were helping out backstage. Thad was with us too. Thad was always with me. He took on Jason's ghost curse and got magically connected to me. When Jason's band members failed to show up at the high school Shana and I had to go look for them and that's when it happened. Shana and I were at this very spot when Thad told us his plans. He said it wasn't fair that Jason got to hog all the glory. He claimed he was going to be a real rock star and that everyone in this town was going help him gain stardom. After his stupid little speech he disappeared along with every single resident of Lakepoint! Everyone was at the school talent show and now everyone is gone!"

Shana nods her head knowingly. "I'm the one who figured out that he's gonna use everyone to be his groupies. Thad is such a weirdo."

"Where was he standing?" Cyclops squeaks.

For a second, I don't know who or what he's talking about, but I clue in pretty quick and jump up. "He got up onto this wall when his ego first started to explode." It's true. Thad had actually climbed this low wall like he needed a stage or a soapbox to shout from.

"Yessssssss." Cyclops hisses from my pocket. "I'm starting to see the remains of his power-trail. Please place me onto the wall, Kate."

I'm not surprised Cyclops knows our names. We were told by the Fates that he knew our story. Why I'm having to repeat it for him now is beyond me, but I must comply if we're going to find every single town member any time soon.

Taking Cyclops out of my pocket I nearly drop him onto the low wall when he immediately starts to expand in size. His girth widens and his height lengthens. I can see the rags he's wearing in better detail now.

"That is so crazy." Shana whispers, backing away. She was afraid of the larger version of Cyclops in the catacombs, she seems iffy around him now that he's getting big again.

Once Cyclops reaches a standing height of at least eight feet —on top of the three foot wall he's standing on— his one-eyed presence in filthy rags is a foreboding countenance indeed.

"Yesssssss." Cyclops peeps with his juxtaposing small voice. His one eye is closed. "I can see Thad now. Take my hands and we'll go."

Shana hesitates, but I move forward quickly. When she sees I'm about to grab Cyclops' hand, she sucks up some courage and reaches out as well.

Together we both grab onto one of Cyclops' extended hands. He straightens his knees and Shana and I are both suddenly dangling off the ground. What happens next is unprecedented. One minute we're suspended over asphalt and the next thing we know we're hanging over the precipice of a very high balcony indeed.

"Aaarrrggghhh!" I scream. Dangling for my life.

"Pull us up!" Shana cries.

Cyclops finally complies. He hoiks us both up over the railing where we plop onto the precarious surface. We're high in the rafters back stage at a massive concert. Lights flash everywhere. Smoke rises and most of all music blares at top volume. I'm surprised I heard Shana when she screamed.

Immediately, Cyclops shrinks. I whip him up and stuff him into my pocket. Shana gestures ahead and I follow her along the narrow walk-way. It's precarious going. I'm having to hold onto narrow rungs. If I'm not careful I'll slip and—

"Argh!" I cry out just as I lose my footing. I'm barely hanging on by my fingertips. "Shana!" I shout, but she can't hear me. Inside my pocket Cyclops shrinks to the point of disappearing.

Oh great. Now what am I supposed to do? I'm about fifty feet in the air and no one's around who can help me—

Too late, I've lost my grip.

There is only air all around as I fall. My limbs grapple for purchase on nothing. I snap my head down and just before I hit the stage a familiar face looks up at me.

Thad.

His black eyes that I know are full of stardust reach into my very soul as I plummet towards the floor.

"Oof!" I cry when he catches me in his arms.

I'm saved. Thad's guitar hangs loosely by his side. I'm in his arms and I've got my hands wrapped tightly around his neck. Lights flash, the crowd goes wild with screams and applause. When next I dare look up I see Jason racing toward us. He drops his own guitar just before Thad realizes what's transpiring.

There's a bright flash of light and suddenly I can't hear anything. I can see though and what I'm looking at is no longer a stadium filled with concert-goers.

We're in a field. Thad and I.

"Put me down!" I screech and Thad drops me on my butt. "Ouch. Not like that!" Scrambling to my feet I push him in the chest.

"Whoa, whoa." Calm down, Kate."

"Don't tell me to calm down." I go to push him again but he grabs my arms and puts me into some kind of body lock grip. Damn but I wish I'd taken a martial arts defense class or something. I can't move. I'm pinned against Thad completely.

"Now, are you going to push me again if I let you go?" He breathes his words close to my ear.

I think I can feel Cyclops squirming around in my pocket. Sure enough, my chest becomes heavy. "I won't push you, but I think he might."

Thad snorts a laugh. "He who?"

Suddenly, Cyclops bursts from my chest, tearing a hole clean through my pocket. He grows twice his size as he flies through the air. By the time his big feet hit the ground he's fully formed at over eight feet in height. "Me, Thaddeus. I will push you down."

"Oh sh—"

Thad doesn't get his swear word out because Cyclops wallops him with a massive fist. I'm driven to the side with Thad from the blow and we both go down.

"What the hell, Cyclops?" I spit out dirt and dry grass once I get my bearings and the dust clears. "You're supposed to be helping me, not bashing me around!"

"Aw, Kate." Thad groans and reaches out a hand toward me. "Why did you have to get that pip-squeak involved?"

"Is he talking about you?" I look up and up at Cyclops at the exact moment Thad's hand makes contact with my arm.

Poof!

The field we were just sitting in vanishes to be replaced by a wondrous sight indeed.

We're in a garage. Thad's garage. The garage that houses green statues. The wondrous —if not terrifying and mind-blowing— aspect, is that the garage is floating in space, just above the Earth's atmosphere.

"Holy fffffffffffffffff..."

I nearly swear but then I realize my brain can't actually digest what's happening. There are no words...

All I can do is sit down onto my butt, hard. Thad is standing next to me on the sturdy and capable cement floor of the garage. The double wide door is raised and open. I'm staring out of the garage at the glowing orb of our planet below.

It's as though we're floating in orbit in a garage shaped spaceship. There's no house attached to this garage. I'm aware of this because the walls are made of glass.

This is either one crazy ass dream I'm having, or maybe all that smoke at that concert was ganja and I'm flying high as a kite right now.

"Did you drug me?" Finally, I've found my words. I still feel dizzy though. When an eight-foot Cyclops goes floating by the left glass wall, my head almost spins off my neck in confusion. "What's he doing out there? Is he dead?"

I'm far to calm for this situation. I'm sure of it. The problem is, I can't seem to muster the energy I need to rid my brain of this baffling fog.

"He's a god, Kate. Cyclops can't die."

"Oh. Yeah. I forgot."

Thad just stands there looking down at me. He smiles and his black hair falls in front of his eyes. "Would you like to have a seat on the sofa? It will be a bit more comfortable." He holds out a hand and for some unknown reason I take it.

Thad lifts me onto my feet. I sit down onto the soft couch. He's right. This is much more comfy than the hard floor.

"Can I go home now?" I mumble, feeling disoriented and more confused than ever.

"Why would you want to go home? There's no one there, Kate. Everyone you know is at my concert."

I nod knowingly. Confusedly. He's right again. How could I have forgotten that everyone's at his concert? I mean, I saw them all there. Thad told me he was taking everyone. Even Shana knew he wanted lots of groupies.

"So now what?" I look at him as he sits next to me on the sofa. "Shouldn't you get back to your concert if you're the star of the show?"

"I would." Thad's eyes are like the walls. Looking into his eyes is like looking straight through his head. The universe is in his eyes, complete with stars just like the ones outside the glass walls of this inter-galactic garage. "But I can't now. Not unless you give me something, Kate."

"Give you what?"

"A kiss." Thad moves closer. His eyes flash with darkness. A gleam shines over the surface where his irises should be. There's someone in there. A person crying to get out.

He's nearly on me now. He said I have to give him something. A kiss. His lips touch mine. They are warm and soft. There's more pressure from his mouth. His lips part. Mine follow. His tongue slides in. Hot moistness and more pressure. He's pressing. I'm pulling. My hand entwines into his hair. This kiss roams through my soul. His mouth and hands push into me. All I know is heat and darkness. I see his black starry eyes, even though my lids are shut.

"No." I barely whisper. "Nooooo." I breathe the word into his mouth. "NO!"

White noise erupts like a screaming banshee into my ears. I push Thad away. Make the screaming stop! Make it stop!

Covering my ears with my hands does no good. The screaming persists as though it's emanating through my every pore. My vision is blurred. The screaming. My skin feels like it's going to melt off my form.

"What's happening to me...? What is this—"

Nothing. The pain is gone. No sound. No screaming. No pain. Just my panicked gasps of terror as I try to catch my breath.

*

I've been lying here on this sofa in space for what seems like hours. My brain won't function properly. I can't think straight. All I can do is stare up at the yucky paneled ceiling. There's a starry universe out there to look at, but I can't find the strength to even lift my head.

Thad is seated next to me. He's leaning over me and talking. I can't decipher his words. It's as though he's speaking a foreign language.

Occasionally I'll work up the effort to look down and out through the glass wall. Yep, there goes Cyclops floating around the space-garage like its own little moon.

If I were to look behind the couch I'd see stacked human and creature shaped green statues. Oh yes. The statues are all there. And I know what lies beyond those statues.

A door.

If I were to leap up off this couch right now, and run through the standing statues, eventually I'd find a small door. And what's on the other side of that door is Mount Olympus.

That's interesting. It would seem my brain can function. I can remember something. I know for a fact that this garage is a doorway to Mount Olympus. Just like my limboland is a gateway between Mount Olympus and the Underworld.

Mental sigh of exasperation.

If only I weren't so confused. I'd be able to walk with my own two legs and get to that door. I'd be on Mount Olympus. I'd find my way to limboland from there and then I could get back to Earth. The mortal realm. My home town where…

Where no one is. Because Thad took them.

I look at him now, leaning over me the way he is, talking to me.

Slap!

I smack him across the face and sit straight up. I know my own mind. The fog is gone from my brain. I can think straight and—

"You kissed me!" I aim to hit him again, but Thad grabs my hand and pins me to the back of the sofa.

"You kissed me back, Kate." Thad growls into my ear. He lets me go and jumps back. There's a lingering grin on his face.

I don't waste a second. Springing with all my strength I flip myself up and over the back of the couch.

Thump.

I land on the concrete floor and spring to my feet. I've only taken two steps back before Thad leaps. He flies over the sofa landing in an easy crouch before I can even fully turn to run.

He pushes forward. I take off, but I'm not quick enough. Thad is on me before I know it. His foot goes out in front of mine. I trip and as I'm falling he latches onto my wrist. I'm spun around. I'm not giving up without a fight though and I push off from the floor.

Momentum carries me and the force of Thad's grip ends up making me sail past him into the window.

Glass shatters. I scream in pain from the force of the collision. My back has just burst through the window and I'm sent hurtling into the void.

My voice snuffs out in the vacuum of space like a candle suffocated instantly under a glass tumbler.

Cyclops is there. He grabs my hand just as Thad leaps from the broken window. When the landscape of space vanishes this time I do my utmost to prepare because I have a feeling we're about to appear somewhere new, yet again.

And in an instant I discover my gut feelings were right.

All three of us land in a heap on a the black shiny surface of a stage.

Music assaults my ears, but it's nowhere near as loud as that ethereal screaming I endured in outer-space. The beat thumps my chest as I crawl out from under Thad and Cyclops. I'm surprised I wasn't fully crushed in the fall. Then again, did we fall very far? I don't know how we've been teleporting to all these strange places, let alone how I've survived each and every transition!

The crowd roars and I'm on my feet. Unfortunately so is Thad. He already has his hand latched around my arm before I even have time to regret it and blink! The stage and the music are gone.

This time, when we appear in the middle of a highway crossroad, I plead with Thad. "Stop! Wait! Please don't teleport us anywhere! I'll do whatever you want. I'll even kiss you again and endure that stupid screaming. Just please don't make us disappear!"

When he moves in I shut my eyes and turn away, bracing myself for another blitz out.

Nothing happens. Thad doesn't touch me.

Daring to open my eyes. I look at him. He's standing about a foot away. It's high noon. The hot sun blazes all around this vast empty wasteland. The crossroads we're standing on is edged on all four intersecting streets by red stop signs. There's not a vehicle in sight on the any of the long straight roads in either direction. Dust flies and puffs into small dust devils at the roadside. There are vast fields of dirt and shrubs as far as the eye can see.

Thad doesn't utter a word. He just looks at me with his dark shadowed eyes. His black hair whips in the wind. My own hair is mostly hanging out of my scrunchy, so I pull out the hairband and let my locks flutter around my face in the breeze.

My jeans are starting to make me feel hot. My plaid shirt no longer has a pocket from when a rapidly expanding Cyclops had ripped through it.

"So." Thad grumbles. "About that kiss you offered..."

Steeling myself, I take a deep breath. "Yes, I'll give you another kiss, but only if you'll tell me what you're doing."

His lips purse thoughtfully. For a moment I stare at them. And then I realize I don't know why I just did that. I mean, it's not like I actually *want* to kiss Thad again. The fact of the matter is, I *have* to kiss him if I'm ever going to get anywhere with the guy. Not *there*, as in a perverted way. *Stupid weirdly betraying brain.* Just home. I want to go home and I want my family and friends to be there when I arrive.

"How about a kiss for a question?"

So now he's bargaining with me. "Fine." I blurt. "But if I think you're lying I get to ask you another question."

Thad looks thoughtful for a moment. I think he's about to tell me to go to hell and blitz us both out of here on some new crazy teleporting fiasco, but then he speaks.

"Deal," he says, not bothering with an offer of a hand-shake to seal the bargain. He just moves in, wraps his arms around my waist and readies his lips with a lick of his tongue. "Let the kissing... ehem." He clears his throat with a low rumble and I feel it reverberate through his chest into mine. "I mean, let the questioning begin... of course."

And so it has begun. A kiss for a question. If I had known Thad wanted this from me when I first met him weeks ago, I never would have allowed him to help us.

Jason will never forgive me.

I'm a lost cause. I want everyone's freedom, but at what cost?

The first kiss is slow and tentative and lasts for about ten seconds before I push Thad away. "Why did you take everyone?"

"Damn."

"That's not an answer."

He chuckles. "No, I was just thinking we should have established rules about the length of each kiss.

"This isn't funny!" I rage. "Answer my question."

His eyebrows flicker over his dark eyes. "I took everyone to kick start my career as a rock star." He moves right back in and plants his lips onto mine.

That wasn't much of an answer and my lips don't yield before I'm pushing him away again. "Why is it so important for you to be a rock star?"

"No."

"What?"

"That wasn't a real kiss. I'm won't answer. Also, here's a tip.

You're not asking the right questions." His lips are on mine again in a flash. His hands are around my waist.

If I'm going to get anywhere with this guy I'm going to have to comply. When we're finished though, I'm going to seriously ask the Fates if there's anything they can do about wiping my memory free of this horrific experience.

Finally, I allow my lips to soften.

"Relax your body too, Kate." Thad whispers into my mouth. "A kiss isn't just in the lips."

I do as he says. Reluctantly. It's not easy being kissed by a boy who has basically kidnapped everyone you know. It's just not right and my body has to conform to his wishes.

"That's better." Thad senses the new calm in my body. His kiss is gentle this time. When he pushes in for more I can't help the way my body reacts. I let him push in. I let his tongue collide with mine. His breathing becomes long and deep as our mouths intertwine with warmth.

When I end the kiss this time I don't push him away, but I rest my hand on his chest to make sure he doesn't try to move back in.

I have to take a moment to gather my thoughts. He said I wasn't asking the right questions. I'm confused. His kisses are so gentle and yet his actions are criminal. You don't just kidnap an entire town! Like Shana said: who does that?

Oh my word. Shana. I hope she's okay. How long has it been since I vanished from her side? Where were we in that instance? I don't even know if it was day or night. And why is it high noon now?

"What time is it?" I tip my head up and look at the sky. The sun burns my retinas and I tuck my head down again.

"Ahh." Thad mumbles. "Now you're getting the hang of it. It isn't any time if I don't want it to be." He starts to move his mouth towards mine.

"Wait. What?" I push him away yet again. "That wasn't an answer! You're talking like a wannabe poet now!"

Thad shakes his head and stuffs his hands into his pockets. "You shouldn't get yourself worked up over every answer I give you, Kate. If you can't accept my kisses we'll be here for an eternity." He kicks a pebble and we both watch it tumble and skid off the roadside. When our eyes meet again he's got a mischievous look in his and a slight grin on his face. "Unless you want this to go on forever."

"Don't be crazy!" I cross my arms and turn away from him in a huff. "That's the last thing I want." But the fight has gone out of my voice. I'm at odds with my psyche within myself. I don't want to get too angry and worked up again or I'll never be able to relax into Thad's stupid kisses. So what did his answer about the time of day mean?

He's close again. He puts his hands on my shoulders and presses his body to my back. It's warm out here in whatever desert this is. Combined with his nearness it's absolutely stifling, and yet I'm not perspiring in the slightest. Shouldn't I at least be breaking a sweat due to anxiety and worry? Well, I'm glad I'm not. That would really hinder my kissing abilities and I need to concentrate on giving Thad what he wants.

For now...

His fingers slide up my neck. He turns my head and leans down. His mouth is on mine and I haven't even turned my body around. He's kissing me from behind. My neck is slightly strained and when he deepens the kiss I realize this angle isn't an awkward one. My breathing intensifies and when the kiss ends this time I don't think it was me who finished it. I'm also wondering when my hand decided to wander up into Thad's hair.

Whipping my hand away I finally turn around to face Thad. I'm not very focused though so I almost trip and fall. He catches me round my waist again and what's strange is that my body lets him.

I haven't asked him a question yet. His face is close to mine. My hands hold fast to his biceps. I stare at the rise and fall of his chest as he breathes. It's as if no time has passed since this kissing fiasco began, and yet, I feel like we've been here for eons.

"*When* did you take everyone to?"

There's a low chuckle inside Thad's chest. "Now that is the right question." With his thumb and forefinger he tips my chin up to meet his dark gaze. His star-filled eyes look jet black against the crystal clear blue sky. His black hair whips in the wind and I lose myself in his voice as he answers. "I took them to my future days as a rock star. I found a way out of my curses through time."

Realization comes roaring into my consciousness.

What also comes roaring into existence is the presence of Cyclops. At least, I think it's Cyclops. Or is it just a giant eyeball? And why hasn't Thad reacted by blitzing us out of here? I don't know if I actually feel grateful for the appearance of Cyclops and his overly enlarged eye. I didn't get to finish asking Thad more questions and now he's just going to zap us away into outer-space or something.

It's not like I'm ungrateful to Cyclops for ending mine and Thad's kissing session, or anything like that. It was the only way I'd get answers from him. I *had* to kiss him!

Suddenly, Cyclops' huge eye shrinks and the rest of his body catches up with its size. He shrinks further until eventually he's like a little ogre doll standing on the dusty road. His hands wave me over and I extricate myself from the strangely still Thad. I pick Cyclops up and hold him in my palm.

"Put me onto his shoulder."

I comply with Cyclops' orders and now the miniature one-eyed being is sitting next to Thad's ear.

"Thad?" I snap my fingers in front of his blank eyes.

Nothing. He doesn't even twitch, let alone answer me verbally.

"He can't speak or move," Cyclops squeaks. "He is in my control now. Sorry I didn't figure it out sooner, but I haven't had to enlarge my eye in millennia."

I don't know how Cyclops does what he does, all I want to know is if doing what he does with that eye will help.

As if anticipating my next question, Cyclops starts to explain everything. "I can see into the mind of Thad's eyes. He's figured out a way to use the curses that he has absorbed over time. He can control things by moving into future days. He has set something in motion that will irrevocably alter the present if we don't stop him. We have to inform Zeus."

Oh no. Oh no, no, no.

This is bad. My emotions are on a rampage now and I'm struggling not to show it.

I knew I shouldn't have trusted Cyclops. Well, I didn't exactly know. It was our only option at the time. Shana and I had found Clotho on Mount Olympus after everyone in town had been taken. She of all the goddesses will not want Zeus to discover what Thad has done. Clotho is busy distracting Zeus right now. She's definitely not going to be pleased if Cyclops shows up and starts blabbing about the very thing we're trying to hide from him!

Disaster. This is a complete disaster.

Clotho wouldn't run the risk of losing her Titan god and I certainly won't allow my family and friends to be thrown into Tartarus again.

What am I supposed to do now?

Think, Kate. And think fast.

I know!

Sighing loudly and overly dramatically, I feign agreement. "You're right," I tell Cyclops. "Zeus will definitely know what to do. I'll take Thad to him through limboland."

Without waiting for confirmation from Cyclops I remove the little beast from Thad's shoulder. At the same time I place my hand onto Thad's arm. I concentrate on limboland and suddenly all three of us are there.

We're floating on a cloud. I'm dressed in red velvet robes. Thad now appears to be clothed in gladiator leathers and even little Cyclops and his rags have transformed into a clean tunic.

"So this is your limboland." Cyclops peeps, not at all bothered by the fact that we're all suddenly dressed like the gods. "Clotho injected your visions into my eye. The gods must be thrilled about the discovery of this gateway."

I'm not about to tell Cyclops that the gods don't know about my private gateway. A gateway between worlds that looks down from the clouds onto Hades Underworld and also to the floating island that is Mount Olympus in the distance.

"Would you like a quick tour of the Underworld?" Why did I just say that? Surely Cyclops will figure me out now. I'm just going to have to go for it.

Cyclops shakes his miniature head but it's too late. I've already pushed Thad off the cloud and Cyclops falls with us. We tumble through the air and I think I hear a little scream from the shrunken Cyclops.

I land on my feet and my red velvet skirt billows up around my ankles briefly. I'm getting used to this place and I feel power emanate through me.

Thad plummets toward the ground and I catch him in my arms. His weight becomes heavier by the second though, so I lay him down on the strange surface of the Underworld.

When I was first transported into Hades' land by Jason, my brain was confounded about the glassy ground beneath my feet. Now though, the opaque surface is going to come in very handy.

It captured my friend Shana inside it before and I'm hoping I'll be able to mimic the effect with Cyclops.

"Sorry about this." I apologize to the one-eyed being right before I betray him entirely.

"What do you mean—"

Cyclops doesn't get to finish his high-pitched question. I push him off Thad and onto the surface of the Underworld. My hand touches the glassy ground at the same time and I concentrate on what I'm trying to do.

"What are you doing?" Cyclops' words become muffled.

It's working. He's becoming one with the glassy surface. Well, he's sort of melting into it and soon enough his little body is fully immersed inside the filmy glass.

"I'm sorry." I apologize to Cyclops again. I feel like such a jerk! I'm the one who sought him out for help and now I'm turning on the little (yet sometimes large) creature. "I can't let you tell Zeus."

"You don't know what you've done." Cyclops' lips don't move under the pale glass, but I hear his voice loud and clear in my mind.

Although, as I get to my feet I swear I do actually see his mouth twitch. And it looks a little bit like a slight grin.

"What did you say?"

But there is no answer from Cyclops now. His tiny face is stony and silent under the glass in which I've imprisoned him. His eye closes and he looks like he's asleep.

"I'll take you out as soon as I've got everyone away from Thaaaaaaaaaaaaaa—"

The very boy I was about to speak to Cyclops about has just accosted me.

"Put me down!" I squeal as one pissed off dude with blacked out eyes lifts me off my feet. My legs pedal through the air causing my red velvet skirts to flutter crazily.

The strangest thing happens next. Thad puts me down. His actions are so unexpected I'm caught off guard and I trip and fall over my heavy robes. I land on my butt and immediately look up at Thad.

He's got his hands over his eyes and it looks like he's in pain. It only lasts a moment though and now he straightens, taking in a deep breath. He extends a hand. I take it and he helps me to my feet.

"I know what you've done." I tell him. "I know how you took everyone from Lakepoint. You have to stop, Thad. Cyclops said you're going to ruin the present."

Oh this is going well. *Way to convince him, Kate.*

Thad smiles a crooked grin. He leans close and whispers into my ear. "If the present sucks so much, why not revel in the future?"

And with that he whisks me into the air on a cloud.

"How did you do that?" I question Thad as we float on *my* cloud in *my* limboland. I mean, it is only my gateway because I accidentally discovered it, but I suddenly feel possessive of this magical private realm.

"I'm a gatekeeper too, Kate. Remember?"

Oh. Yeah. Thad and his gateway garage into Mount Olympus. How could I have forgotten? I am so stupid. I didn't think when I'd pushed him and Cyclops here. I just knew I had to stop Cyclops from informing Zeus about our activities. I didn't stop and think about revealing limboland to Thad. Now who knows what he'll do with the ability to travel between realms?

That mischievous grin is back on his face as we float in the air.

Oh great. Please don't tell me he's going to force me to kiss him again. I go to push him away and I'm once again surprised when he lets me go.

Maybe he's coming around. Maybe he'll let everyone go and everything will be normal again. If I can just get through to him, but how best to go about doing that with a guy who seems bent on becoming a superstar?

Through his ego, of course! I'll placate his pride.

"I have more questions," I tell him straight up. "If it means I have to kiss you again for answers, then I'll do whatever you want."

"No thanks."

"What? Oooohhhhh!"

Without warning Thad scoops me into his arms. One minute we're floating on a cloud and the next thing I know we're dangling over a balcony.

My surroundings come into focus gradually.

I'm no longer wearing robes of the gods. My top is the pocket torn plaid shirt, I'm wearing my skinny jeans and my feet are clad in my simple black ballet flats.

Thad isn't dressed as a gladiator either. His t-shirt is black. His jeans are black. His biker boots are black. His long hair is black and his skin is pale in sharp contrast to the black starry nothingness of his eyes.

He sets me down and I finally recognize where we are.

"Shana!" I shout when I see my best friend. She's sitting on the same platform Thad and I have just materialized onto.

"Kate!" Shana jumps to her feet and makes her way toward us.

Suddenly, the platform starts moving and I look down. We're high in the backstage rafters. Sound bursts into my senses and the roar of a crowd nearly knocks Shana off her feet.

I call out to her as Thad simply looks on with that annoying smile on his face. My voice is drowned out by pumping music. Shana manages to grab onto the railing as she steadies herself.

Lower and lower the platform drifts until my eyes are blasted from all angles by lasers and multi colored spotlights travelling around and around in dizzying patterns.

We're at a concert venue that must be housing tens of thousands of screaming fans.

My family and friends are amongst the crowd. I know it. Everyone from Lakepoint is here. Where we are —or even *when* we are— I have no idea, but it doesn't matter now because it appears that I'm about to become part of the show.

When the platform touches down the crowd roars with even more excitement. Thad drops to the stage, raises his arms and the crowd goes wild.

I look at Shana through the dizzying lights and pumped in atmospheric smoke. Grabbing her hand we jump off the platform together as it starts to ascend back up into the rafters.

From out of nowhere Jason appears holding two electric guitars. His blonde hair shines under the moving spotlights. His black ensemble of t-shirt and jeans is so unlike him. What's strangest of all are his eyes. They're surrounded by darkness, but it's a painted on persona.

My boyfriend is wearing eyeliner.

It's not too much makeup actually. He looks like a rock star. My heart punches into my stomach as Jason walks right past me without a glance. He hands one of the guitars to Thad and together they both strum a blaring electric chord off their steel-strings at the same time.

The cheering and screaming of the concert crowd is becoming unbearable. My hand is still clasped in Shana's grip as Thad turns to me. I hear his voice inside my head and suddenly I lose control of my legs.

I think Shana's under the same influence too. Together we both start moving back into the shadows of the stage. We're behind the drummer now and the show begins.

There's nothing I can do. I'm rooted to the spot like a tree that's been implanted into this stage for centuries. I watch as Thad and Jason put on a rock show that blows my mind. As out of control as this situation seems, a part of me is reveling in the music and the atmosphere. I'm overwhelmed because I can't control my movements. My senses are overloaded and all I can do is stand here and endure.

It's a good thing Shana is here too, otherwise I think I'd really lose what little control I have left.

Although, that sense of control flies out of my mind when the show is over. Thad and Jason performed one song. Thad turns around and I can barely see him from this distance. I know he's looking at me though because his eyes control what happens next.

Poof!

Shana and I blitz out of existence. When sight returns to me it's as though nothing has changed. We're still on a stage. Shana is by my side, but one thing is different. She's not holding my hand. Instead, she's dancing and swaying in time to the music.

I'd call out and ask her what she's doing, but my mouth won't work. I look back towards Thad again and my eyes flash.

Now everything is completely different. We're backstage in the dressing rooms. Jason is sitting on a plush sofa and Thad is leaning casually onto a long makeup table. It's against a wall of mirrors that are lit up around the edges.

The worst thing of all is that both Jason and Thad are surrounded by girls. One of whom is facing away from me as she smooches the hell out of my boyfriend's lips.

"Oh no you don't!" I scream and run forward. Grabbing a wad of the girl's blonde hair, I yank her off of Jason. "Shana?" I cry, when I see her face. "What are you doing?"

My best friend just smiles at me. I let go of her hair and glance up at Thad.

I shouldn't have done that. His starry dark gaze overpowers my mind. He flashes a smile. Then the grin is wiped off his face. His inner emotions seem at war within himself. One minute he's smiling darkly and the next his features seem tormented.

He seems to regain control of himself and all the egotistical madness returns to his posture. His biceps strain the sleeves of his black t-shirt. I watch, unable to tear my gaze away as two girls slide up to him. Their hands peruse his taught torso, smashing his t-shirt onto his skin. They pull at his top as though they each want a piece of him.

Without taking his dark eyes away from me, Thad kisses one of the girls.

My own lips react. I don't know what's happening to my thoughts. I look on as he kisses the other girl, all the while keeping his gaze locked onto mine.

Flash!

We're catapulted into another concert.

Flash!

Music pumps and we're at another venue. Crowds scream. Jason and Thad perform like true rock stars.

Flash!

We're in another dressing room. Bodies writhe. Girls everywhere. Smiling at me. Sweaty bodies dancing to the beat that thrums all around. The headiness is infectious. I'm sweating. I'm hot and bothered with the dizzying transportations.

Jason kissing girls. Thad kissing girls. Me dancing with my best friend. People everywhere.

Dancing. Concert going. After parties. My life is a party. I am a groupie. All I know is music and dancing and bodies and writhing and kissing and partying and...

Days are endless. Is it night time? All I want to do is dance. All I want to do is kiss the boys.

I lock lips with Jason. There are lights all around. Dancing girls all around. I see Thad's eyes as I kiss my boyfriend. I watch Thad. I kiss Jason. My boyfriend deepens the kiss and together we breathe each other in. My eyes never close. Thad nears. I pull away from Jason. Our foreheads touch. I breathe even more. He breathes. Our breath mingles.

Senses on overload.

Thad is here.

Jason is here.

I pull them both to me. We all lock into a three-way kiss. Two tongues lap at my own. Lips part and suck and close and lick. My libido kick starts my heart into my throat. My eyelids shut and all I know is heat. My mouth becomes enflamed with warmth. My mind bursts and spills confusion into my eyes as tears.

Wetness soaks my cheeks just before my face flashes and I'm blasted away from the kind of kiss I never dreamed I'd experience.

*

"Kate?" Shana croaks.

There is only the sound of her voice.

Sight returns to me and I'm aware of my surroundings.

No more music. We're in the dressing room.

The silence is broken by a scream from Thad.

All the girls present start screaming too. They rush out of the room nearly trampling Shana and I in the process.

"Jason!" I go to him now that I'm in my right mind.

Everything is steady. I'm not a crazed-out lunatic with no control.

My boyfriend takes me into his arms for a quick embrace. "What's happening to him?" I cower into Jason's capable presence as Thad continues to scream and scream.

Shana just looks on, staring as though she doesn't know what to do.

Thad's screams have an ethereal countenance that starts to affect us all. It terrorizes our ears, but most of all my brain starts to unfold.

There's nothing any of us can do but look on as Thad's agony becomes ten-fold.

Suddenly, the screaming stops.

I'm left gasping for air and I can see Shana and Jason are in no better shape. It's as though we've all been drained by Thad's suffering.

He's holding his face. When his hands lower it's Shana's turn to let out a scream.

Thad has three eyes.

"What's happening." I feel like I can move now. I take a step forward, but Jason pulls me back.

"Wait." He tells me. "It's okay."

I don't know what to do. I watch as Thad's features become strained. His third eye is in between his two black eyes. It blinks open and I recognize it immediately.

"Cyclops!" I cry out.

Thad slaps his hand over the third eye that's on his forehead. He pulls in an outward motion and something incredible starts to happen.

Light pulses between his hands and the third eye. "It's coming out!" Shana shouts and points at Thad.

She's right. Thad is pulling out the eye with the light that's emanating from his hands. It pops free of his forehead and Thad throws the eye onto the floor. It rolls away and stops at Shana's feet. She barfs all over it and then promptly passes out.

My own head feels dizzy and grossed out beyond belief. I can't quite digest what's happening. Bile rises in the back of my throat. I see the eyeball blinking up at me, slightly splashing vomit out of its iris with each flap of its lid.

I too lose control. There's nothing else I can do really. My senses were overloaded long ago and I welcome unconsciousness. I faint dead away and I don't know if I'll ever be capable of waking again.

*

When I do wake up I don't want to. Memories come flooding back to me and I stuff my head under my pillow.

My pillow?

How the heck did I get into my bedroom?

Sitting bolt upright I look around.

Yep. I'm in my bedroom. I'm wearing my SpongeBob Square Pants pajamas and matching pink Patrick socks.

I know better than to presume my memories were in fact a dream. And so, creeping out of bed I leave my room and head down the hall.

"Good morning!" Dad boasts as I walk into the kitchen. "Wasn't that an ace show by your boyfriend last night? Your mom really was wrong about you not dating that god."

"Richard!" Mom throws a slice of toast at my father.

"Dad?" I rub my weary eyes. "Are you talking about the Lakepoint High talent show?"

"Duh." My own father mocks me after taking a huge bite of previously flung toast. With a mouthful of burned bread he continues to embarrass himself. "Rock on! Jason's band totally kicks ass!" He does a fist pump in the air with his pinky and index finger extended.

Mom rolls her eyes and I cringe inwardly. "Just eat your toast. You haven't been a teenager for thousands of years. I hope you're not planning on having a mid-immortal crisis."

"Ha!" That actually makes me laugh. Only someone like my mom would have to worry about her godly husband having something that must be way worse than a regular old mortal mid-life crisis.

Ding dong.

The doorbell rings and I leap at the chance to answer it.

Hurrying to the front door I whip it open to find Thad standing there. He's looking at me and I'm staring back at him with my jaw hanging wide open.

"You're eyes." I point at his face. "You're eyes." I say again, flabbergasted. "They... they're black... but they... they..."

"They're normal, yes." Thad finishes my sentence for me.

It's true. His eyes are real eyes. They're normal eyes. I can't tell where his pupils end and his black irises start because they're all the same color, but the fact of the matter is.. they are real eyeballs. Complete with surrounding white spheres.

"Can I talk to you for a minute, Kate?"

His words do not compute. I'm too busy being amazed by the sight of his eyes. They are stunningly black and I can see that he's looking at me. He's looking me over. He's checking me out by roaming his eyes up and down over my... my...

"Oh my Sponge Bob!" I slam the door in his face. How could I be so stupid? I answered the door wearing the most childish and glaringly yellow pajamas I own.

What an idiot I am!

After raging at the ceiling with silent fists of fury for exactly ten seconds, I open the door once again.

"Come in." I pull Thad bodily by the scruff of his black t-shirt. "Sit there and wait." I show him into the front room and then I hurry off to change. After throwing on a t-shirt and jeans and brushing my teeth, I walk back towards the front of the house.

"Okay, spill." I tell Thad, plummeting onto the soft bouncy sofa next to him. "I want to know everything that happened after I passed out. I can't believe I fainted, but I did so you're gonna have to spill the beans. Where's Shana, and where's Jason?"

Thad takes a deep breath and then slowly releases it. "Your friends are at home. It's where they've been all night. They don't remember anything because I've wiped their memories. I can do the same for you as well if you'd like me too, Kate."

Whoa. Whoa. Whoa. "Are you telling me Shana and Jason wanted you to take away their memories?"

Thad shakes his head. "I didn't ask them."

"You what?" I jump to my feet, outraged. "How could you do that to them? What if they didn't want you to do that? How do you know Jason doesn't want to remember how..."

Oh boy. I've run out of steam in an instant. I've just realized I don't want Jason to remember what happened because what happened was I kissed Thad. A lot. What also happened was that I kissed Thad while kissing Jason at the same time!

"You were saying?"

Thad looks at me with his amazing new eyes as I flump onto the sofa once again. Now my arms are crossed and I'm fully pouting. He's right. Jason and Shana shouldn't have their memories of last night. What does it matter anyway? Clearly everything is fine. No one in town knows they were abducted. My parents are back to their usual selves. Especially my dad. If my dear father knew Thad was here right now he'd burst into the room and say something embarrassing.

I've got to get Thad out of here as quickly as possible. "So why did you do it? Why did you kidnap everyone in town?"

"I didn't. Cyclops did."

Say what?

I don't interrupt, I just let him explain. It's a little strange looking at him with his normal eyes and he's going to have to explain those babies to me as well. I'll make sure he does so.

"Cyclops entered my mind's eye last night. I was aware of his presence in the catacombs from the moment I stepped foot into this town. There are many curses I've taken on for Medusa over the years. There are things at work in Lakepoint that are best kept secret, Kate. I thought Cyclops was held safely away in the catacombs, but I was wrong. He orchestrated last night's fiasco. He put thoughts into Clotho's mind on Mount Olympus. All of it was him. And I can prove it."

Thad reaches into the pocket of his jeans. He pulls out a slender piece of opaque glass. Trapped inside is the shrunken Cyclops.

"You cut him out of the ground in the Underworld?" I gasp.

Thad nods. "I took him after pushing him out of my mind."

I gasp again, shocked beyond belief. "That's what happened last night? That eyeball was Cyclops? The one that Shana barfed on?" That is one memory I know my best friend would be grateful at having lost, if she knew it was taken from her in the first place. "But did it all happen last night?"

This time Thad shakes his head. "No. Cyclops has been using my abilities to shunt us into the future. I had all of his hopes and desires inside my head. I barely had control over my actions. He wanted to exist as a superstar in the mortal realm. He was captured and locked away in the catacombs thousands of years ago for his atrocities against mortals."

There's only one thing I've mainly picked up on. "You didn't have *any* control over your actions at all?"

He looks at me. His normal eyes gleam with intensity. "I had full control over every kiss I asked you for, Kate. It was the only way I could try to reach you. It was me who told you that you were asking the wrong questions."

I don't know what to say. My face is burning with embarrassment. "So it's not like I was kissing Cyclops, right?" I blurt nervously. I look down at the miniature one-eyed creature. No wonder Cyclops had smiled at me when I'd trapped him in the glass of the Underworld. He knew perfectly well that he was going to inhabit Thad's mind anyway.

Shivers run down my spine at the thought of the manipulation. I feel guilty too. I shouldn't find comfort in the fact that it was Thad who kissed me every time. I shouldn't be kissing anyone but Jason!

I don't know what to do. Should I tell Jason everything that happened. What about Thad's eyes? Before I know what I'm doing I've reached up toward Thad's face. "How?" Is all I say.

"I pushed out my curses into Cyclops' eye when I tore him from my mind last night." His smile is sheepish. "I'm free, Kate. And I have you to thank for it."

He leans in and presses his lips to mine. For a moment I don't respond. My eyes are wide in astonishment. Is this right? Should I let this guy say thanks to me by giving him a lingering kiss? He has been cursed for a long time. I guess he's just really, really grateful to me...

Slowly, I push him away. "I'm sorry, Thad. I..."

My hand is on his chest. His breathing is hard and deep. "I know, Kate." He whispers. "You're with Jason."

Nodding my head I don't look up at him. I just let him go. He rises from the couch and I remain seated. I'm not going to look into his stunning black eyes because I don't know what I'll do if I see the way he looks at me.

I am grateful to him as well. He will know what to do with the captured Cyclops. Everyone in town is safe. My boyfriend doesn't know what transpired and there's no need for me to tell Jason anything that would hurt him. I'm never going to kiss Thad again. It's as though every kiss I shared with him never happened.

The front door opens and then I hear it click softly shut.

Thad is gone and I'll never allow myself to look into his new eyes again.

STORY V

Dream Come True

Funny. I don't remember Thad having snake skin instead of normal human flesh. Also, I don't recall him being fifty feet tall.

But apparently that's what he is, at this juncture in time. He looks like a guy with green skin of a scaly snake. His height soars over most buildings on Main Street, and he seems to be abducting all the teenage girls in town, simply by scooping them into his hands. The pockets of his jeans and shirt are positively brimming with overflowing girls.

They don't seem to be all that upset with the situation either.

As a matter of fact, all the pocketed girls look downright pleased that Snake Thad is carrying them off to who knows where.

"Hey!" I screech at the top of my lungs, shaking a fist into the air. "Thad! What are you doing?"

Stomp, stomp, stomp. Thad the snake dude wanders away from me. No matter how loudly I rage and cry out, he pays me no mind. It's as though he's deaf to my puny existence.

"Whatever." I decide to stop following him when he's wandered far away enough that he looks a normal size. "If he wants a collection of girls then what do I care?" Scuffing an angry toe against the tarmac, I run away in the opposite direction. "I mean, it's not like he's my boyfriend or anything!"

I'm actually running so fast now that everything flies past me in a blur. Tears stream from my eyes and I don't know if it's because I'm crying or because the cold wind is stinging my irises so greatly.

"What do I care? What do I care?" I scream out loud and in my fury I don't notice when a great big tree jumps in front of me, smacking me across the face with one of its branches.

*

"Kate! Wake up!"

Someone has hurt my face. Someone is yelling at me.

Blinking my eyes open reveals that someone is my mother.

"Heavens above, Kate!" She gasps. "You were screaming in your sleep!"

"I was?" Sitting up blearily, I rub my eyes to find them wet with tears. "Sorry, Mom. I must have been having a nightmare."

"What was your dream about?"

Yawn. "I don't remember."

"You don't...? But how can you not remember a dream that would make you scream that loud? You were chanting something about not caring..."

"I was?" Another yawn. "Weird."

Mom swipes my hair back off my forehead.

"I'm tired. Can I go back to sleep now?"

"Are you sure, Kate?"

"Yeah, I'm fine. Just so tired. I don't even think I'll dream this time..."

And that's that. My head hits the pillow and I'm out like a light. As I drift off to sleep once again I'm aware of a brief moment of remaining consciousness. Just enough time to wonder why I can't seem to stay awake. It's as though I'm going into a deep coma. Maybe I shouldn't have let Mom allow me to fall back asleep. But how exactly was I supposed to stop that from happening?

*

"What's with all the cop cars at Amy's house this morning?" I ask my best friend Shana when we arrive at Lakepoint high school in the morning.

"At Amy's too?" She frowns deeply after placing her books into our shared locker. "There were tons of cop cars at Michelle's, I saw them on my way here."

I stop, book poised just before the locker shelf. "Uh oh."

"What oh?" Shana grabs my book and stuffs it into the locker before slamming the door shut.

"Two incidents with the police and you haven't thought to wonder?"

"Don't say anything." Shana walks away.

I catch up with her and block her path. "So you do know what I meant by *uh oh*."

"You never know." Shana pretends to brighten. "This could just be a coincidence."

A couple of Juniors walk by gossiping loudly about more police cars being called to residential homes.

"Did you hear that?" I stare Shana down. "The cops are everywhere this morning and what do you want to bet none of those girls will be in class today?"

Shana sighs loudly. "I know what you're thinking, Kate. But this might not have anything to do with the gods."

Shana is completely wrong. I know she is. It has everything to do with the gods. When something goes awry in this town it always has something to do with the gods and/or goddesses of Mount Olympus. Either them, or the Titans of... well... Lakepoint town.

That's what my hometown is. Home to the Titans who used to be trapped in Tartarus. All any of the gods of Lakepoint want to do now is live peaceful lives with their mortal partners. When you're dealing with otherworldly powers though, things do tend to go a bit haywire.

Especially when the offspring of gods discover they have magical powers.

I have to wonder if that's what's happened to the girls who are clearly missing from school today.

"See? Told you." I whisper to Shana as we enter homeroom."

"Just because Michelle and Amy aren't here, doesn't mean it's something to do with—"

Before she can finish her sentence of denial, the wall screen blinks on and the principal's face comes into view. "Miss Carter, can you please send Kate to my office."

That wasn't said as a question. I've been called to the principal's office on a Monday morning and it's not even nine o'clock.

"Never mind." Shana sighs loudly, taking her seat at a shared double desk. "This probably does have everything to do with the gods."

I don't know if I'm pleased she's finally agreeing with me, or if I should be worried that even she knows there's probably going to be trouble ahead today.

*

"Umm... you wanted to see me?" I poke my head into the principal's office.

"Yes, Kate. Please have a seat."

Principal Euphrasia has a strange enough name to make me wonder if she's a Titan goddess, or if she's married to one. Her black hair and striking light gray eyes follow my every move as I enter the office and sit down in a chair facing her desk.

"Ehem." Principal Euphrasia clears her throat. "It has come to my attention that you're familiar with certain goings on in this town, Kate."

I am?

I can't help but wonder what certain goings on she's alluding to.

"Your parents have informed me that you're friends with a boy named Thad."

Oh. Him. "Yes, I know him. I wouldn't exactly say we're friends..."

Principal Euphrasia squints her eyes, questioningly. "More than just friends then?"

"No!"

Oops. I blurted that a little too loudly and half jumped out of my seat.

Settling back down, I calm myself. No one but myself and Thad knows what happened a short time ago. No one else knows about that kiss we shared. A kiss that was also shared with someone else.

Feeling a lot of embarrassed blood creeping up my neck, I quickly reply. "I mean, no we're definitely just... I know Thad because he's Jason's friend."

"Ah, I see."

She sees what? I wonder.

"So Jason is your boyfriend. That is a problem."

It is?

This is news to me.

"Why is my love life a problem to you?"

I get another scowl with her probing gray eyes for that remark. Then, Principal Euphrasia sighs loudly. "I'm sure you're aware of the situation with the Olympians and the Titans, Kate. Your boyfriend being an Olympian is the exact reason I've chosen to contact you, instead of him. I know you must support your father first and foremost. He's a Titan, after all."

Okay, clearly this woman knows everything about the gods and goddesses. I'm pretty sure at this point she's not just a regular mortal woman either.

"So you're a Titan."

Principal Euphrasia nods her head in confirmation. "I am."

"And you don't want my Olympian boyfriend to know I'm meeting with you."

Another nod from the Principal.

"Why?"

"Because, Kate." She gives me her most critical stare down yet. "Your other demi-god boyfriend has kidnapped some of our students."

*

"I take it you got bad news at the Principal's office." Shana looks at me as though she's concerned. It's lunch time and we're both sitting under a tree in the common area outside.

"How did you guess?" I ask her rather dryly.

"Well, your face looks gray."

Oh great.

Maybe Principal Euphrasia stared at me long enough that my skin took on the hue of her eyes. I wouldn't be surprised to find this was true. I have no idea what powers goddesses and gods are truly capable of.

Such as it is though, I don't think my current pallor has anything to do with irises reflecting off my skin. No. The reason for my obvious state of distress is because of what Principal Euphrasia asked me to do.

"She said I have to find Thad."

Shana frowns. "Find Thad? Why? Where's he gone to?"

"I don't know, and neither does Principal Euphrasia." Sighing loudly, I get to the point of the matter. "I have to find him because he has kidnapped some girls."

"He what?" Shana balks.

I nod my head. "Yep. And apparently he did it while covered in snake skin after having grown to fifty feet in height."

Now Shana really blanches. "Are you kidding me?" She nearly screeches. A couple of students nearby look at us briefly, so I tell her to keep it down.

"Why does it matter if I shush?" Shana says, not too much quieter. "If Thad is a fifty foot tall snake man then people will notice. Why hasn't Principal Euphrasia found him? He can't hide being a gargantuan monster. What am I saying?" She shakes her head. "Why do you automatically believe the Principal about this anyway?"

It's my turn to frown. "Because." I mumble under my breath. "I've already seen him looking exactly like a fifty foot snake-skinned man."

*

I told Shana about my dream. She didn't even bother not believing me. Well, she'd tried to deny it for about two seconds, but then quickly gave up when she saw the seriousness in my eyes.

Now that the school bell has rung and we're on our way home, Shana bounces on her feet excitedly beside me. "So when are we going to get Jason? I wonder what magical power stuff he'll do to find Thad the snake monster."

"Don't call him that." I don't know why I suddenly feel defensive of Thad. "And we're not telling Jason anything."

Shana stops bouncing and walks normally beside me. "Why not? He's a freakin' demi-god, Kate. He could probably snap his fingers and make SnakeThad appear before our eyes. Or his dad could—"

"His dad is exactly why we can't tell him. Hello? Do you want my dad to be sent back to Tartarus if Zeus finds out about this?"

"Oh yeah." Shana mumbles thoughtfully. "I forgot about that.... but why did Principal Euphrasia tell you to find him?"

Sighing loudly I angrily kick a pebble on the ground. "Because she's convinced I know him well. She thinks he's my boyfriend."

When Shana doesn't immediately reply, I look at her. "What?"

"Nothing." She raises her eyebrows.

"That face doesn't mean *nothing*. What are you thinking?"

"Well, you do like Thad as more than just a friend. I can totally tell."

What's going on here? Did Thad tell Shana about the crazy kiss we shared?

"Have you been talking to Thad behind my back?"

"What?" Shana cringes visibly. "No! Why? Would it matter if I did? What would he tell me?" She winks at me and I'm tempted to shove her into a nearby bush. Only gently, of course.

"Very funny. Let's just concentrate on the task at hand, okay?"

Shana shakes her head. "I can't believe Principal Euphrasia is like totally leaving this all up to you."

"She's not."

"Huh?"

"She wants both of us to find Thad, and we have to keep it a secret. It's the whole reason she's told me to do this. She doesn't want word getting out and then Zeus finding out about it."

"She told you to tell me?"

Tilting my head, I reply sheepishly. "Not exactly."

Shana stops walking so I do as well. She folds her arms. "What do you mean?"

"Well, I told her that if she won't let me tell Jason, she'd have to let me tell you, at least."

Now I get a scowl from Shana. "So you dragged me into this because you're a meanie, not because it was Principal Euphrasia's idea."

"Pretty much, yeah."

Shana shakes her head in dismay. "I'll get you back for this."

"No you won't."

"I won't?"

"Nope."

"Why not?"

"Because you love it."

Another scowl on my best friend's face. Then, she relaxes and smiles. Skipping away ahead of me, she calls out loudly. "You're right! I do love it! Now let's go find your snake man boyfriend!"

I've created a monster.

I'm not calling Thad a monster. I'm referring to my exuberant friend.

What happened to the cowering girl I once knew who jumped at the sight of a spider?

Well, I can't complain that she's toughened up. We both have. How could we not, by now? We've been through so many weird magical ups and downs this past year, I'm beginning to wonder if it will ever be possible to regain a normal life some day.

After making a Pringles ring of chips, then eating the entire container at my house, Shana and I head to my room. So how are we going to find Thad if we don't tell Jason?" She bounces onto my bed.

Hmmmm... that might be a problem. Thad lives with Jason. They're roommates. Jason's parents don't even live in this dimension, so he's ultra-cool having a place of his own on Lakepoint Drive.

"I'm guessing Thad isn't there anyway." I sigh loudly and sit next to Shana.

"Well, duh." She replies. "If the Principal knew where Thad was, she wouldn't have told you to find him."

"Or would she?"

Shana frowns. "What you mean?"

"Well, we don't know for a fact that what Principal Euphrasia told us is one hundred percent true. She could be lying."

"Why would she do that?" Shana's brow is really crinkling together now.

"I don't know. It's totally weird, but I think I dreamed about what happened to Thad and those girls."

"You what?" This astounds Shana so grandly, she jumps up from the bed. "Why didn't you tell me that?"

Shrugging my shoulders, I keep calm. "I'm not completely sure I did dream about Thad."

Shana giggles.

"Not like that!" Now it's my turn to rise to my feet. "I didn't *dream* dream about him. Besides, no one can control their dreams."

Shana looks pensive. "Come on."

"Where are we going?" I ask her as she takes my arm and pulls me out of the room.

"We are going to find out for sure if Principal Euphrasia is lying or not."

"Wait." Stopping in my tracks, I reign Shana in. "We can't tell anyone about this. We can't just show up at Jason's asking for Thad, remember?"

"We're not gonna ask Jason."

"We're not?"

"Nope. We're going to sneak into his house though."

And with that statement Shana turns abruptly on her heel and heads straight outside.

*

By the time Shana and I get to Jason's house the sun has set. We took a detour and stopped off to have coffee at a cafe. I'd told Shana at the time that we were in a hurry, but her crush was there so she just *had* to have a hot drink, so that she could stare at him the whole time.

We're sneaking around the back of Jason's house now and I'm getting scraped by bushes galore. I've been busy, and distracted, thinking about how to get Ben to ask Shana out. That way I won't have to go on stalking missions with her any longer. It sure is boring sitting around staring at a guy your friend likes.

"Ouch!" I cry out in a whisper yell when an extra sharp thorn scrapes my arm. "This is stupid."

"Well, you do what you gotta." Shana whispers back. "Stop being such a wimp."

Rolling my eyes doesn't reveal my contempt. Shana can't she can't see my face very well in the darkness.

Thirty minutes later and we're both starting to get fed up. "This is pointless," Shana complains. "It's not like we can see into every window to find out if Thad's here, or not. Besides, I'm cold and getting bitten by too many mosquitos."

So much for the new found sleuth in my best friend. One night of staking out a place and she's ready to call it quits.

Now that's the real Shana I know.

Yawn. "I'm bored too. Let's start again tomorrow."

When we get back to my place Shana and I are immediately accosted by my parents. "You've had ten million messages from your school principal, " Dad says. "I know, I counted them all."

"Your father is exaggerating again." Mom crosses her arms. "He's not far off the mark though. Euphrasia, amongst others, is desperate to get hold of you. Did she call your cell phone?"

I shake my head and yawn some more. "No messages on my phone... and what do you mean by *others*?"

"The parents of the missing girls, of course." Mom looks daggers at me.

So. She knows. "I thought Principal Euphrasia wasn't going to bring you in on this."

"She didn't really have a choice, now did she?"

I think Shana can sense the tension in the room. "I'm just gonna go home now," she says sheepishly, before vacating the premises.

Great. Thanks for the support my so-called best friend.

"Can we deal with this tomorrow, Mom?" I yawn doubly loud. "I'm just so frikin tired."

Both of my parents are frowning at me now. Dad looks concerned, but Mom looks put out. Finally though, her frowny face subsides. "Yes well, it's a lot of Euphrasia to ask of you. I don't know why she didn't tell us in the first place."

"Get some beauty sleep, honey." Dad kisses my forehead and

sends me off to my room, but not before leaving me with an unwelcome remark. "I could pack an entire suitcase into those tired bags under those eyes."

Charming.

He's right though. I look into the mirror on my vanity table before my head hits the pillow on my bed. I look pale and drawn. My eyes have dark circles under them, indicating a lack of sleep. Come to think of it, I don't know if I've had a full night's rest this entire year. It's just one mystical thing after the next in this crazy town.

Well, I'm not going to get sleep by worrying about my awful complexion. So I make immediate contact with head upon pillow and within a matter of seconds I'm out like a light.

*

At least, I thought I'd drifted off to sleep. I'm wide awake now though, and staring into a slightly familiar night darkened abyss.

This is limboland. *My* limboland. Only, it's currently occupied by someone other than just me.

"Kate?" A boy's voice calls to me. I can just about make out the outline of a body through the cloudy haze, because that's where I am right now. Limboland is in the clouds. It's a place between worlds. From where I sit on billowing fog I can see Hades Underworld below, and in the distance ahead is the floating island of Mount Olympus.

"Who are you?" My voice sounds ethereal in my throat as though it's as light as the surrounding clouds.

"It's me, Dillon."

He walks into view, stepping out of the fog. His legs are sunk into the cloud up to his knees, but I can clearly see he's not dressed in a modern style, without having to see the gladiator sandals I'm certain are on his feet.

"Dillon?"

It is him. The boy I met in the Underworld earlier this year. The demi-god, like me.

He sticks out his hand. I take it and he helps me to my feet. "What are you doing here?"

"I'd ask you the same thing." He quirks a crooked grin at me. "I didn't think anyone else had access to this place unless I brought them here."

He what?

"Wait. What are you talking about? This is my place. It's my limboland and only I can bring people here. See?" Twirling, I let him peruse my Grecian goddess style gown. "Whenever I visit limboland it re-dresses me into fancy togas."

Dillon raises an eyebrow curiously. "It changes my clothes for me too, Kate." Letting go of my hand he sweeps his arms down his personage in a show-off gesture. Which isn't' necessary. I can already see he's dressed like an ancient Roman prince.

"Well that is weird. I thought I was the only one who could come here."

Dillon nods. "I thought that too... about me."

We stare at each other for a moment. Clouds billow and swirl around us. It's night time and intermittently I can see twinkling lights shining from Mount Olympus in the distance.

"So what are you doing here?" I ask Dillon.

"I was just going to ask you the same thing. I went to bed just now and woke up here. I don't normally come here unless I know about it first." He grins and winks at me. I forgot how cute this guy is. He's about six foot tall, like Jason and Thad. His hair is dark brown and cut short and neat. I know for a fact he's a demi-god, because Dillon helped us when I first discovered that I too was a sort of demi-goddess.

Shaking my head makes Dillon frown. "Are you okay?"

"Sorry... yeah." I look up at him. "I was just thinking about how we met, remember? We both thought we were dreaming in the Underworld. It turned out to be real and now here we are, floating on a cloud of magic. Life just got weird when I met you."

Dillon chuckles. "You're not wrong about that, Kate! And *wow* did things get even weirder after our little road trip."

Weirder?

I'd forgotten about the road trip. Jason and I had taken to the road with Dillon to drive him home, across hundreds of miles of country, after the Underworld fiasco. "What do you mean?"

"Well." Dillon raises his eyebrows. "You're not going to believe this Kate, but my whole town is populated by Titan gods and goddesses."

I'm floored. I mean, I would be if I were anywhere near the ground. What I am exactly is astounded beyond belief. "Are you being serious right now? Because there are Titans living in my home town too. My dad is a Titan god!"

Dillon's eye's go wide. "Is that why we were able to do what we did in the Underworld? I remember you saying stuff about demi-gods."

Feeling overwhelmed, I sit on a cloud. Fog puffs up around us when Dillon sits next to me. "I thought the Titans were all living in Lakepoint after their escape from Tartarus, but you're telling me there are more of them where you live?"

"That is so weird." Dillon shakes his head. "I thought all of the

Titan gods and goddesses were only in my home town. It's been so crazy when a kid finds out they're a demi-god. We've had a lot of trouble at home with new found superpowers going to kid's heads."

Will the revelations never cease? "That's exactly what's been happening in my town! A few months ago Medusa's daughter discovered her powers and she gave me snakes for hair!"

"Seriously?" Dillon turns to me. "Another senior at my school found out his mother was the goddess Eos! He blinded me with weird sunbeams from his hands during football try-outs. I almost didn't make the team cut until my best friend and I figured out how to stop him."

Smacking my forehead, I lay back in the clouds. Twinkling stars surround my vision and I can tell the night sky is clearing up. "That's crazy dude. So crazy." I can't think of anything else to say. I'm trying to comprehend what this all means.

Then, something dawns on me. Sitting bolt upright once again, I nearly smack foreheads with Dillon. I didn't realize he was watching me. "Does Zeus know about the Titans in your town?"

"You mean the bearded guy who used to be stuck to one of your shoulders?" Dillon laughs a small laugh.

"Yeah, that guy." I roll my eyes.

"Not that I know of. Although, he's like the god of god's, so he probably sees everything, right?"

Shaking my head, I'm adamant. "No he doesn't. Trust me, he's too busy with Mount Olympus politics most of the time. Besides, I don't think it would be a great idea if he *did* find out about the Titans in your town."

"Why?"

"Because that might make him panic. He knows about the Titans in my town and if anyone steps a foot out of line, Zeus always threatens to send them back to Tartarus."

"Oh."

I nod sagely. "So if he were to find out about your Titans, he'd probably go ape shit about it and send your parents, and most of the adults you know, back to Tartarus too."

"Oh. Whoa." Dillon stands. The clouds at his feet have almost entirely evaporated now. There are stars everywhere and I feel like I'm floating in outer space. "That's probably a big deal, isn't it?"

Getting to my feet, I nod. "Yeah. As much as my parents annoy me sometimes, I wouldn't want them sent away forever."

"Me either. I guess I should probably tell my parents that Zeus knows about your town."

"Yeah, you probably should."

"I'll tell them right now. I'll be right back." Dillon squeezes his eyes shut. When he opens them, he looks surprised to still be in limboland.

"Something wrong?" I ask him, feeling like I know the answer.

"I should have just vanished out of here just now." Dillon frowns in all seriousness. "Come to think of it, how did I get here in the first place? I don't remember wanting to be here."

"Same." I look around quickly. "Last I recall I went to bed and then woke up here." I squeeze my eyes shut and think about returning home. When I open my eyes again I'm still in limboland. "Uh oh."

"You stuck?"

I nod in reply to Dillon's question. "I should have zapped out of here too, but it didn't work. Maybe we can fly..." Stretching my arms upwards has no effect. Jumping up and down in this big billowing dress is awkward and doesn't get me anywhere either.

"Oh crap." Dillon mumbles.

"Very crap." I agree.

I think we're stuck here.

*

It's been thirty minutes since Dillon and I realized we're both stuck in limboland. During that time much pacing of sparse clouds has occurred. We've tried everything we can think of to get out of here, but nothing works. I've stomped on clouds, he's tried throwing himself off the cloud's edge. All that transpired from that little experiment is him whirling back into limboland and crashing right into me.

Luckily, clouds are very soft to land on. Awkward, lying underneath a very cute demi-god who isn't my boyfriend, but not all too uncomfortable.

Dillon rolls off me and we just lie there. Thinking. At least, I think he's thinking. I'm definitely thinking about our predicament, because it's cold up here. When he notices me shivering, Dillon pulls me close.

"What are you—?"

"I can't seem to get warm either, Kate. Is this okay? Sharing body heat?"

Sighing loudly I have to acquiesce. "Yeah, it's alright. I guess. But this is strictly for survival reasons. I have a boyfriend, so don't try any moves." I have to laugh at my audacity. I mean, it's not like Dillon likes me or anything. Although, we did share a moment up here in limboland not too long ago...

"Don't worry, Kate. Like you said, this is strictly for survival. We wouldn't want to die of hypothermia in between worlds, now would we?"

*

Another half hour passes and I almost drift off to sleep. Almost.

The second before I zonk out, I realize something. "What were you doing before you got here?" Pushing out of Dillon's arms, I sit bolt upright.

"Oh. I thought you said you were cold."

"I am, but we've got to figure this out. We can't just lie here together forever."

"Why not?"

I look at Dillon funny.

He smiles and sits up too. "I'm just kidding, Kate. What's on your mind?"

That's a strange question, considering the fact that getting out of limboland is the only obvious matter on my mind right now. I'm not certain how much Dillon's kidding around about lying here with me for an eternity. He doesn't seem in a hurry to vacate the place.

"What were you doing before you appeared here in limboland, Dillon?"

Yawning, he rubs an eye. "I think I went to bed and then bam! Here I was."

"Me too!" I blurt, getting to my feet.

Dillon joins me in standing, but he's not pacing the clouds like I can't seem to keep myself from doing.

"So what does that tell us?" Dillon sounds tired and not very enthusiastic about resolving our current predicament.

"Well, if we both fell asleep just before we got here, then maybe…" I stop pacing and round on him. "Maybe we need to fall asleep again to get out of limboland!"

Dillon smiles. "So we should lie back down the way we were?"

I'm momentarily taken aback. He's saying we should cuddle in the clouds again. "Well no." I finally admit. "We don't need to do that. Actually, it would be bad if both of us fell asleep at the same time."

"Why?"

"Because we don't know what might happen."

"Oh. Yeah. Sure. You're right."

Frowning, I ponder his short cut words. I don't think he's very hopeful about my plan. "Umm... do you want to try falling asleep first? I can ummm... wait to make sure you're okay."

"No, no." Dillon quickly interjects. "It's fine. You go to sleep first and I'll keep watch. If you vanish after falling asleep then I'll now you're idea worked and I'll try to get some shut-eye too." The smile that follows his diatribe is wide and cheesy. A little too enthusiastic in nature, but what do I know? I just want to get out of here and back to Lakepoint.

I shouldn't have fallen asleep in the first place. Principal Euphrasia and the parents and friends of those missing girls were desperate for my help. I can't believe I let myself fall asleep like I did. I just couldn't seem to help it. I felt absolutely comatose by the time I'd gone into my bedroom!

"Okay thanks." I take Dillon up on his offer. I really am desperate to get home now. My motivation fuelled by a bit of guilt. "I just hope I can fall asleep now with all this worry."

Dillon chuckles slightly. He sits next to me as I lie down on the cloud and close my eyes. I relax as full as possible, letting my thoughts wander. Except, every time I'm about to doze off, I'm rudely awakened by Dillon either coughing, sneezing or making some other sort of bodily noise. I just hope he's not planning on farting in my general direction in the next fifteen minutes, because that seems to be how long it takes for me to drift into dreamland before he wakes me all over again.

Sitting up, I sigh in despair. "This isn't working. You're going to have to move over there." Pointing a finger I indicate the direction of the floating island of Mount Olympus.

"I am?" Dillon gets up, brushes cloud fluff off his tunic and looks down at me.

"Yes. You're too noisy and I can't sleep."

"Sorry."

Dillon does look truly apologetic as he wanders away. Only once he's almost the size of a dot in the distance do I give him the thumbs up that he can stop walking the clouds. I notice he sits down and that's when I lie back down.

Finally, and quite quickly, I drift off to sleep.

*

It worked! I'm back in Lakepoint. I think. Or do I think? Why did I want to be home anyway? And why did I want to be in the middle of town?

I find myself walking along Main Street, with small one level stores and local businesses on either side of the road. That's the only familiar thing about this place though. There are no cars parked along the curb. There's no traffic either.

Something is wrong.

Or is it?

The time of day must be sunrise. So where is everyone? And why am I walking anyway? I don't seem to be able to control my leg movements. They're like heavy anvils and each step I take booms down into the asphalt.

Boom, boom, boom go my footfalls, growing heavier and louder with each step until finally the ground is quaking beneath my feet.

Correction. The ground is shaking beneath the massive feet of a fifty foot Thad.

He's back.

He's here.

He's walking towards me and the closer he gets the more I realize he's still at least fifty feet in height. Also, his skin hasn't returned to normal. He is like a snake dude with green scaly flesh.

My legs have finally stopped moving me towards the great monster of a man, but Thad certainly hasn't stopped booming his gigantic feet towards me.

I can't move. I'm rooted to the spot. The closer Thad gets the more detail I can see about his huge personage.

The girls! He's got the captive girls from town sticking out of his pockets. They're all screaming to be let go. Thad even has hold of five girls in one hand and probably five in the other. I don't know. I can't count while dreaming.

That's it! I must be dreaming and now that I know this I can force myself to wake up. Right? Isn't that how dreams work? Once you know you're in one you've got full control.

Bang!

Thad brings one of his mighty scaled fists down onto the low roof of a Main Street building. He has no regard for the girls in his hand. Each of them go flying, landing in the rubble that was once an intact store front.

"No!" I scream as though I'm shouting through air that's thick as honey.

The girls aren't moving. They're just lying there either injured or...

I don't want to think about the other option. Clearly I am not in control of this dream. If, in fact, this is truly a dream.

"Thaaaaad!" I scream again with a thick drawling voice. He's about to crash his other fist into the ground and I dread to think what will happen to the girls he's holding. "Stop!" I yell and wave my arms.

He catches sight of me and drops his raised arm.

Well, that was a mistake. Thad is now immediately running towards me. In three giant footsteps he closes the distance between us.

I still can't move. My legs won't obey the commands I'm shouting at them from inside my head.

When he arrives Thad stops for a moment, looking way, way down at me. His eyes gleam with intensity. I return his gaze, having nowhere else to go.

Suddenly, Thad throws his head back and lets out a loud roar. The girls in his captivity all scream even louder. The noise becomes overwhelming, almost unnatural. I push my hands over my ears to try and block out the horrid sound.

It doesn't work.

The screaming reaches a crescendo and one by one every window in the buildings along Main blow outwards, exploding over the sidewalks and into the street.

Glass rains down and sprays horizontally into my skin. When I take my hands away from my ears I find blood on my palms.

There's blood everywhere. Small gashes in my flesh are blossoming across the fabric of my clothes. I could have been cut to ribbons if I'd been standing any closer to those windows.

The screaming continues. It's overwhelming me. I go down on bended knee, but I look up at Thad.

At his huge foot, to be precise, because he's just raised it over my head.

He's going to bring it down on me and squash me like a bug. I'm doomed to die like so many insects I've accidentally stepped on and for some reason the only worry that's on my mind at the moment is; if I get out of this alive, I promise to tip-toe everywhere I walk from now on.

Poor bugs. I know how you feel in these my last moments of existing.

And now my own screaming ads to the cacophony. I scream and scream until I feel the beginnings of pressure on the top of my head.

Thad is pressing his foot slowly down onto me and my bones will surely be crushed any moment now...

*

The pressure has changed to shaking. My eyes are squeezed shut tight. I don't know what's happening to my body. I feel queasy, like I'm going to barf any minute now.

"Kate, wake up!"

My mother's voice penetrates the fudd that is my mind.

Blinking my eyes open I find her leaning over me. Her hands are on my shoulders and it's her who's shaking me quite violently.

"What the...?" My voice shudders. "Mom! Quit it! I'm awake!"

"Oh!" Sorry, honey." Mom releases my shoulders. "It's just that your eyes kept opening and closing. It's like you were in a coma!"

"Well I'm definitely nowhere near sleeping now. Why did you

wake me up?" I yawn.

With a great big flourish, Mom stands and wrenches the blanket off me. "You want to know why? I'll tell you why, young lady. You were screaming bloody murder in your sleep about a giant snake boy and the phone has been ringing off the hook! Get up, Kate. We have to go."

"Go?" Groggily I shift up onto my elbows. "Go where?"

Mom sighs loudly as she heads out the door. "To save the town from your boyfriend, that's where!"

Wow. Talk about *not-enough-information*. I have no idea what my Mom is saying. I'm so tired and it's taking me a while to fully wake up.

Then, realisation dawns.

Snake boyfriend. Phone calls. Me screaming in my sleep.

A horrific nightmare comes flooding back into my mind.

Thad.

Kidnapping. Building wreckage.

Fallen girls who didn't get back up...

And Dillon!

Why has his existence popped into my mind?

Something to do with my limboland. *His* limboland?

Mom's right. I really do need to get out of bed. And so that's just what I do. I hop up and get dressed in a hurry. I'm out of my bedroom like a shot and standing in the livingroom a split second later.

"What's happening, Dad? What are you...?"

My words trail off because basically there are no words for what I'm witnessing. My father is beclothed in shining gold armour. He looks like a god of Olympus wearing a white gladiator tunic beneath a gleaming chestplate.

And he's holding a sword.

An actual sword.

A very long, wide and stabby looking sword that shines brighter than the armour he's wearing.

"You really do have a sword." Finally, I can speak. "So you were serious when you wanted to chop off my head."

Dad's face is a picture that confirms my suspicions. "Well yes, darling. You had snakes for hair, at the time. Chopping off your noggin was a great idea."

My father arcs his sword through the air a few times. It makes otherworldly swishing noises and I swear the thing is trying to sing.

"Be careful with that!" Mom comes bursting into the livingroom. "I don't want any of my sofas getting chopped in half again."

"Your sofa?" I blanch at my mother. "What about my neck? My own dad is insane. He wanted to kill me!"

"Oh don't be so dramatic, Kate." When Mom says this Dad winks. "Your father was never going to cut off your head because he realized you're a demi-god and not a full goddess of Olympus, right dear?" She glares at Dad.

"If you say so, darling."

"Dad!" I blurt at the same time Mom yells, "Richard!"

She turns to me. "Forgive your father, Kate. He was a Titan god for millennia. He doesn't know a lot about this mortal parenting thing."

"Hey, woman." Dad points the tip of his sword downwards. He looks dejected.

Sighing loudly, I go to him and pat his metal encased shoulder. "Chill, Dad. It's okay. You've done a pretty good job so far."

"I'm about to do even better by you, my darling daughter." His face lights up. "I'm going to slay the mighty snake beast and save you from your own destructive boyfriend!"

Before he can start swishing his sword around again, I correct him adamantly. "He's not my boyfriend. And you probably shouldn't exactly slay him... like... dead, or anything."

"Why ever not?" Dad's face is a picture of confusion. "He's out there destroying the town—"

Suddenly his words are cut off by loud booming sounds in the distance.

I don't need telling twice. Dad's right. Thad really is causing a lot of damage. And I think I know why he's doing it.

"Just don't kill him please, Dad!" I call after my armour wearing father as he bolts out the front door. "It's my fault he's a giant fifty foot snake dude!"

***

Mom and I run into town. We don't have to take the car, it's not far until we locate the source of destruction along Main Street.

"What did you mean back there, honey?" Mom runs alongside me and she's a little out of breath. "Why would you think this is your fault?"

"Because I dreamt it."

I don't have to see her face to know she's frowning in concentration. I don't have time to look at her face, actually, because we've arrived at a scene of utter chaos.

He's here.

The gigantic Thad standing fifty feet tall with skin covered in green scales. Seeing his image in reality is worse than any nightmares about him combined. The metaphorical wind is knocked from my lungs, and I haven't even fallen over. It's the sight of him that's thrown me for a loop. All the destruction he's causing has me momentarily grounded in shock. I can't move a muscle because I can't believe this is happening.

"Kate!" I hear someone scream my name. As if in slow-motion I look to my right as Shana comes charging towards me. What's also heading in a collision course with my body is a car.

I assume this has been thrown towards me by the very large snake-skinned Thad.

There's only a split second to let this register on my mind before Shana throws herself into me, knocking me sideways into my mom.

We both manage to escape maiming by a car having been hurled at high velocity.

Landing on my side hurts and I grunt in displeasure. At least crashing to the ground has woken me from my shocked stupor.

"Are you okay?" Mom asks me and Shana. "Let's get you two out of harm's way."

Scrabbling up onto our feet we duck around the end of the row of buildings that line Main Street on the West side. Mom peeks around the edge of the brick wall and I have a look to see what's happening too.

It's incredible. A sight to behold. There are Titan gods all standing and fighting at Thad's feet. Some of them have teenagers who I go to school with. All of them are wearing the same type of golden armour my Dad is sporting. They all have gleaming weapons too, most of which are swords, but I swear one of the Titan goddesses was wielding a golden mace.

The Titans who don't have weapons don't seem to need them.

They have bursts of light and strange emanations of power flowing right out of their hands.

All of their actions are aimed towards Thad as he smashes his way through town.

"They have to stop him reaching the residential areas!" Mom yells. "Everyone's been evacuated from this street, but I dread to think what he'll do to the towns people if they don't escape their homes soon."

This is bad. Really, really bad. And it's all my fault. I've got to do something to help!

The one thing I've gratefully noticed is that monster-sized Thad isn't in possession of any screaming teenage girls. I don't know if this is a good thing though. I'm hoping it doesn't mean he's dropped them somewhere.

"I have to stop him!" I round the edge of the building just as mom reaches out for me.

"Kate, no!" She screams, but I'm already heading towards the main source of danger; big bad Thad and his awful new green skin complexion.

Waving my arms and shouting at the top of my lungs, I look up trying to get Thad's attention. "Down here, you great big snake man! Look at me! It's Kate!"

I think it's working. Thad has stopped smashing buildings and throwing cars around. His attention has been drawn downwards.

The Titan gods are still throwing everything they've got at Thad, but they don't seem to be having an effect on him. Their swords and powers have managed to scuff his shoes a little, but that's about it.

What is keeping his gargantuan form from falling to the powers of the gods?

"Thad! You have to stop what you're doing. This isn't your fault!"

"Kate!" My father stops cutting slashes at Thad's thighs when he sees me. "Get away from here!"

"No, Dad! You don't understand. This is all my fault—"

My words are cut short when Thad bends low. I don't think he's aiming to pick me up though, because his hand is in the shape of a fist.

Shit! He's going to squash me, just like in my dream, except with his huge fist and not his massive foot! I'm doomed…!

The fist of fury doesn't make contact with my personage. I've shut my eyes, waiting for the impact that never comes. When I open them again I can see why.

Many of the Titan gods and goddesses haven't been successful at blasting Thad with their powers, so they're now using their abilities on the next available resources. There are cars and trucks being hurled through the air at Thad's head. Finally, he's backing away. Blow after blow, magically thrown vehicles pummel into him.

What have I done? Is Thad going to die as a fifty foot monster? How did my dream of him, in this form, come true in the first place?

"No!" One of the Titan goddesses screams. Another Titan has been kicked into a nearby building by Thad.

He's fighting back and because of his great size he seems to be winning.

"We have to keep him away from the residential neighbourhoods!" Dad yells.

All of the Titans double their efforts, but it's no use. Thad is too big and too strong. He pushes forward while we all back away. Eventually I'm forced to join Mom and Shana beside the corner of the building once again.

"I have to warn the towns people, but I want you to get Shana out of here, Mom."

"Screw that!" Shana takes off and I pelt down the street after her.

"Shana wait!"

"I have to make sure my family are okay, Kate. You go and warn everyone else."

"Kate!" Mom catches up to me, running alongside. "Evacuations already started. There shouldn't be anyone in the closest houses to Main Street, but I'll check to make sure. You just help your friend."

"Are you sure, Mom?"

There's really no time to argue. Once she nods her head in confirmation the two of us split off running in opposite directions.

I just hope Shana's parents were informed about the evacuation too. I don't know what we're going to do if Thad should reach any homes with people still inside.

*

I catch up with Shana just as she's stomping up the front porch steps to her house.

"Mom! Dad!" I hear her shout from within, once she's flung the door open. "We have to get out of town! There's a monster on the rampage!"

She doesn't get an answer from her parents, but she definitely gets some words from me. "Shana, your parents must have evacuated like my mom said. Have you called them yet?"

Reaching into her pocket, Shana pulls out her phone. "Good idea. I'll call them right now."

I can hear loud booming noises in the distance, growing closer by the second. "Maybe you should dial on the run. I don't think we should stick around here for too long. Let's head towards the lake.

Thad isn't moving in that direction."

Shana stops dialling. "I can't just leave without knowing where my parents are, Kate. What if Thad has already eaten them, or something?"

Okay, now she's being crazy. I didn't see Thad eat anyone in my dreams. Although, he does look like a snake, so maybe anything is possible. Even the most horrific of outcomes.

"Thad hasn't eaten anyone."

Shana looks up and I turn around at the sound of a voice in the open doorway.

It's Shana's mom, Phoebe, and she's wearing golden armour. Her blonde hair seems to be glowing as brightly as the long staff she's holding in her hand.

"Mom?" Shana gasps. "You... you..."

"Yes, Shana. I'm a Titan goddess." The golden woman steps into the house. As she does it seems like more magical wind blows her hair around. She looks like the most beautiful super hero I've ever seen. Especially with the way her fist is perched on her hip. "I didn't want you to find out about me this way." Phoebe adds. "In fact, I had intended to keep my true identity a secret from you forever, if that were possible, but I can see it is not."

Wow! She even talks like someone sent here to save the world.

"Let's get you two out of here before—"

Bang!

All of a sudden Shana's house collapses in on us.

Dust and debris flies everywhere but for some reason we haven't been crushed. When the first blast of dust settles I can see a car amongst the rubble that was once Shana's livingroom. Above us stands Phoebe with her staff held high. There's some sort of protective shield emanating from it to encase all three of us.

That's why we weren't crushed. Shana's goddess mother saved our lives!

When the next big bang happens it takes the remaining roof off of the house. I can see Thad approaching swiftly, all the Titans at his feet useless at stopping him.

I don't know what to do. Any second now Thad will be on top of us. The loud bangs and crashes must have deafened me because I can see Phoebe's lips moving, but I can't hear what she's saying.

Whoosh!

Suddenly, the protective shield we're standing under vanishes.

Phoebe moves quickly over the barely settled rubble that was once her home. She runs toward the approaching Thad, shouting at everyone to get out of the way. Just before he's within stomping distance Shana's mom stabs her golden staff into the grass at her feet.

The ground begins to rumble so violently outwards from where she's standing, Thad is knocked off his feet. The rumbling continues and the ground opens up.

It's swallowing Thad whole! He's being submerged in dirt and before I can even blink he's sunk down into the earth completely.

Phoebe continues to hold her staff to the ground. The rumbling has lessened, which means everyone can stand and approach her.

Shana and I run for it. "Mom! You saved us!" She tries to hug her mother, but finds it tricky with all the hard golden armour she's wearing.

"We're not in the clear yet, dear. I don't know if I can hold him down there forever."

Shana and I look at each other and I'm pretty sure her face

reflects the same worried look as my own.

I know what I need to do. At least, I know what I need to try.

"Shana!" Grabbing one of the strewn bricks off the lawn, I hand it to my best friend. "You need to hit me over the head with this right now."

"Say what?" Shana looks at the red brick I've just given to her. "What are you talking about, Kate?"

"I have to fall asleep to fix things, but I don't really think I can just doze off at the moment. You're going to have to knock me out so I can dream all of this away."

There's still that confused look on Shana's face, and she hasn't raised the brick to knock me unconscious.

"Seriously, Shana... you need to—"

"That won't be necessary, Kate." Phoebe is still holding tight to her shuddering staff as it rumbles lowly in the ground. "Your parents are here."

Mom and Dad both run towards us. Mom is breathing heavily from exertion, but Dad isn't huffing and puffing in any way whatsoever. Do gods and goddesses even need to breathe at all?

"Do you really know what's going on here, Kate?" Phoebe asks me, snapping me out of my strange revere.

I nod in confirmation.

"You'll have to put your daughter to sleep." Shana's mom looks at my mom.

"What's happened?" My mom says. "How long has Shana known about...?" She points at Phoebe's golden armour.

"I've known for about two minutes that my mom is a Titan." Shana steps forward and holds out the brick in her hand. "But we don't have time to talk about that right now, unless you want me to konk this onto your daughter's head like she asked me to."

"She what?" Dad looks quizzical. "So you don't like my neck slicing ideas, but you'll let your friend bash in your skull?"

"Oh, Dad." This isn't the time for his weird ways. I pinch the bridge of my nose in frustration. "You don't understand. I dreamed about Thad being a gigantic monster. I met Dillon in limboland and I fell asleep and now Thad is in the ground..."

Huffing out a breath of frustration I stomp on the rumbling ground.

"Just trust me when I say I need to sleep right now."

Mom is on it. "We do trust you, darling." She whips out a glowing golden string from her pocket, and an equally as shiny golden pin too. I'm just relieved she didn't whip out her magical scissors. My mother retains the powers of the fates. One snip of the string she's holding and I'm toast. Dead as a door nail. She's holding my personal timeline in her hands. "Now, let me just pinpoint your consciousness on your timeline and—"

The moment mom sticks the pin into the golden string, I feel myself falling. My body is crashing to the earth and my consciousness is fading into dreamland.

I hope.

*

It worked.

I think.

I must be dreaming.

Everything is hazy.

Now, to control my subconscious. I must not slip into a deep enough sleep where I forget myself. I have to dream the right thing. I've got to dream Thad back to normal so that he can be released from inside the ground.

Wait just one minute.

This dream state really is foggy. I can't see a thing. How am I supposed to control what I'm dreaming if I can't see what's going on in the slightest?

"Stupid clouds." Fanning my hand through the air, the fog begins to clear.

Ah. That would be why I didn't quite feel asleep. It's because I'm wide awake and in limboland.

"Dillon?" I call out to the boy I know I left behind when I'd last zonked out. "Are you still here?"

"He's here all right. And you're going to stay here too. Forever."

That definitely wasn't the sound of a boy's voice. It was definitely female in origin.

"Who is that?" I get to my feet, poking my head out the top of the clouds.

I was right. There is a girl here. She's dressed like a goddess wearing a blue toga-like gown. Her hair is long and black as a raven's. It's nearly down to her knees. If I weren't so confused right now, I'd have time to be extremely jealous of her beauty. Also, I don't need to see my body under this curtain of cloud to know that I'm probably dressed in ancient Greek apparel too. Such is the way of limboland. I swear this place is haunted by the archaic fashion police ghosts, or something.

"Who are you?" The obvious question for the strange girl spills automatically from my lips. "How did you get here?"

"I hitched a ride with dream boy here." She waves her hand downwards and the fog clears all the way down to her feet. Lying there in a pool of swirling mist is Dillon.

Stepping out from behind puffy clouds, I go to him and lower myself on bended knee. The velvety skirts of my white toga gown pool in the mist. "What happened to him? Why did he bring you here?"

"Because he loves me."

I look up at the girl who's stunning enough to be a beauty queen.

"Oh... umm... okay." I reply, not knowing what else to say. "So you're like... his girlfriend?"

She grins wickedly at me. "Not exactly... yet... but I will be, or else..."

Or else what? I wonder. And that's a really weird way to say she'll soon be Dillon's girlfriend. A threat?

"So do you want to help me wake him up?" I ask the strange pretty girl.

"Now why would I want to do that when I'm the one who put him to sleep?" She tilts her head and looks slyly at me. "How have your *dreams* been lately, Kate? Or should I ask you how your *nightmares* have been?"

Okay. So she knows who I am, and she knows about my dreams. Alarm bells have long since gone off in my head.

"Dillon!" I bend and scream in his face. "Wake up!"

His eyelids flutter, but he doesn't fully wake because the pretty girl —whom I have decided is also insane— has grabbed my hair from behind.

"Yeow!" I shout, flailing my arms behind my head. "What the hell are you doing?"

"You can't wake Dillon now." Insane-oid Girl bends and hisses in my ear while still gripping my hair. "The best part of his dreams are about to come true in your town."

Oh no. What's that supposed to mean? Now I'm sure I need to wake Dillon more than ever.

Lashing out with my legs, I kick Dillon just enough to shake him. "Wake up Dill—"

I don't get the rest of his name out of my mouth. Crazy Girl has hauled me to my feet by my hair, which really hurts. She whirls me around and bodily throws me across the plane of clouds. Skidding across fog isn't exactly painful, but I'm going to be useless at waking Dillon from this distance.

Who is that bonkers crazy girl anyway? And why is she doing this? The more I look at her now, the uglier she becomes on the inside, thereby distorting her supposed pretty outer features.

As soon as I move towards Dillon, Crazy Girl accosts me again. She's up in my face in a split second. She presses her palms to my temples and immediately I start to feel very tired.

"Sleep, Kate." The girl intones. "Sleep and dream of monsters until they come alive and destroy you."

What the...?

Punching both arms up through her's, I open my fists and shove both of her hands away from my head. "Screw that!" I scream and dive. I'm lost in cloud cover and I creep along the foggy surface.

"Where are you, you bitch?" Crazy Girl hisses. "You're all Dillon has talked to me about, month after month. I'm going to destroy you so that he pays attention to me for once!"

Destroy me? Sheesh.

I take back what I thought about this girl earlier. She wouldn't be a beauty queen, but she definitely qualifies for best drama queen ever.

Finally, I reach Dillon. "Wake up please, Dillon. I shake him while still hiding under the clouds. At least, I thought I was hidden enough. In a flash though, Crazy Girl's hands are back on my temples.

I'm surprised when she doesn't continue to scream at me, but then her words register and I suppose shouting wouldn't exactly work with what she's attempting to accomplish.

"Sleep, Kate. Sleep forever." She groans and it takes all my strength to resist.

Giving one final shove at Dillon, I absolutely screech his name. "Dillon, wake up!"

He wakes, sitting bolt upright as my consciousness begins to fade.

"What's going on?" Dillon looks from me to Crazy Girl. "Kate!" He tries to dislodge her hands from my head, but it's no use, I'm falling fast. "She's Wisteria, Kate. Think about her mom, the goddess Asteria. Call to Asteria, Kate. Keep calling to Asteria..."

And that's all I now know. The name of Asteria. It floats through my mind as I drift into a forced coma.

*

I'm dreaming. I know I must be dreaming. Keep concentrating on the dream and I won't think I've slipped back in to reality.

Asteria. I must remember that name. But why? I don't know.

Asteria. Think of her name. Who is she? What did Dillon say?

Wisteria?

No. That's not the right name.

Asteria only.

Asteria...

Asteria...

Asteria...

*

"Hello?"

A woman's voice speaks to me.

"Hello." It says again. "Wake up girl. You've come to me by the power of dreams. Now isn't the time to remain comatose."

Well that's woken me up.

My eyes blink open and I find myself staring into the face of the crazy beautiful girl again. Only she looks a bit older.

"Who are you?" Crazy Older Girl asks me now. "How did you how to find me through your dreams?"

Gazing around quickly, I take in my surroundings.

I'm inside the kitchen of a perfectly normal looking modern household. The woman before me is dressed in jeans and a t-shirt, and she's got a knife in her hand.

"Don't stab me!" Backing away I hit a nearby window. I'm still brain fuzzled and I don't know if I'm dreaming or not.

"Don't be silly," the woman huffs and sets the knife down onto the countertop, next to some vegetables she was just chopping up.

It's obvious to me now. She wasn't going to stab me.

"Sorry." Sighing heavily, I rub my temples. "Could you tell me if I'm awake?"

"Of course you're awake." She reaches out and pinches my arm.

"Ouch." I cry out and rub the sore spot.

"See?" She adds. "You're awake. Now will you please tell me what you're doing here?"

"Wisteria."

It's the first name that bursts from my lips.

"What about my daughter? Is she in some kind of trouble?"

"No... what? You're Wisteria... right?"

The woman glares at me. "I'm not Wisteria, I'm her mother

Asteria."

Oh. No wonder she looks so much like that crazy girl in limboland. I'm assuming that's who Dillon meant when he said the name Wisteria—

"Dillon!"

Realization dawns.

"Your daughter! She's crazy!" My eyes bulge. "She's got my friend! I was supposed to think about your name... I..."

I thought I was starting to figure things out, but my head is now confused all over again.

"Slow down and stop making wild accusations for just a minute." The woman orders me to sit down on a chair at the kitchen table. She looks down at me. "Now I know you must at least be a demi-goddess as you've managed to appear using your dreams. So would you please explain carefully what happened?"

She's right. I need to calm myself. I need to think clearly about what's going on.

"You're Wisteria's mother?" I mumble.

She nods. "I'm the goddess of dreams. I assume your arrival here by dream is what drew you to me."

"Yes!" I stand, making this Asteria woman take an astonished step back. "That's what Dillon said. Something about dreams! We've got to save him! Wait!"

I immediately panic all over again. "We have to save my home town!"

Asteria places her hands onto my shoulders and shoves me back down into the chair. "One thing at a time please. Now.. shall we start with your name?"

"Kate." I pant, a little hysterically. "I'm Kate."

"Alright, Kate." She says soothingly. "Where did you come from just now?"

"Limboland."

That answer doesn't get a reaction from Asteria, so I continue. "Limboland is the place between the Underworld and Mount Olympus. Just trust me on this. Your daughter is there and she's got Dillon captive. I know this sounds dramatic, but it's true. And I'm pretty sure your daughter is the one who made my nightmares come true. The Titans in my home town are trying to hold my boyfriend... I mean... he's not my boyfriend..."

Why did I just say that? Jason is my boyfriend, not Thad!

"... a guy named Thad — he's a demi-god — or maybe he's a god. Whatever he is he's now a fifty foot dude with scaly snake skin who the Titans are trying to hold underground."

There. Done. I've said my piece. Now the question is; will this stranger believe me?

"Damn." Asteria swears. "I guess this means my daughter has discovered her powers, and not in a good way."

"No." I shake my head. "Definitely not good. Not good at all."

Asteria sighs loudly and stands straight. "Okay," she says with authority. "Here's what we're going to do. We'll get you to the Titans in your town and stop whatever nightmares of yours' have come true. Then we'll go to this limboland you speak of, and I'll deal with my daughter from there. Sound good?"

"Sounds great!" I hop up onto my feet and blurt, "let's go! But it will have to be limboland first, or I won't be able to get to Lakepoint!"

When Asteria looks at me quizzically, I explain that I have to think about limboland to get there, and then from that in-between place I can think myself back to my home town.

"It's the only way!" I'm getting very anxious now. All this talking is costing time and making worry. Is Thad still being held underground? Is Dillon okay with Crazy Girl in limboland?

"There's another way." Asteria looks at me with her big gorgeous eyes. "Like I said, we should really go to your town first—"

"Why?" Frowning, I question her motives.

"Because... Kate, is it?"

I nod in confirmation that Kate is my name.

"Well, Kate. I really think I should be allowed to speak with my wayward daughter on my own after seeing to whatever mess is occurring in your town."

Fine. I guess she's entitled to that. She is the crazy girl's mother, after all. Although, I wouldn't mind sneaking in at least once face punch to Wisteria's pretty head. She's caused a lot of trouble for me and I don't even know who she is!

"All right," I acquiesce. "We'll do it your way... ummm... what exactly is your way?"

"Through dreams, of course."

Oh no. Not that. Anything but that. If I can help myself, I'm determined to never sleep and dream again!

I think Asteria has noticed my hesitance by the severe shaking of head I'm doing.

"I'm guessing my daughter has used the powers of dreams on you." Asteria looks depressed. "She's going to be in so much trouble." Her teeth are gritted, but she calms herself. "You can relax though, Kate. You won't even know you're asleep before we're there. Now, what's the name of your home town?"

Pursing my lips, I eventually agree. There's nothing else I can really do. "Lakepoint." I tell her the name.

"Good, now concentrate on that place." She puts both of her index fingers to my temples.

Something sleepy happens inside my body for about half a second and suddenly we're there.

"Whoa!" I stumble and back away from Asteria's touch. "You weren't kidding. That was really fast. Did I even fall asleep?"

"For a brief time." Asteria looks around. "So... this is one of my fellow Titan's towns."

One of? What's she saying? "Exactly how many Titan towns are there? Wait. Never mind. I'll ask you later. We have to get to my friend's house."

Or what's left of Shana's destroyed place of residence.

"Thad is trapped underground, but I don't know for how long—"

Boom.

Something bangs in the distance and the ground rumbles. Asteria and I seem to have appeared on a children's playground. I know where we are and it's not far to Shana's house.

"This way!" I yell to Asteria before taking off on foot at a running pace.

We don't have to travel far before the source of the noise comes into view.

A filthy, dirt covered Thad is still fifty feet tall, and he's obviously escaped the confines of the earth he was forced down into by Shana's mom.

"Oh no! He's out!" I panic and skid to a halt, Asteria stops beside me.

"Wisteria!" She screeches suddenly into my ear.

What's going on? I told her that her daughter is in limboland, not here in Lakepoint.

"Wisteria!" She screams again and I can see that I was so wrong in my assumptions.

Her daughter is here.

Wisteria is walking in front of the gigantic Thad. She's with Dillon and they're all three heading our way.

Upon finally hearing her mother's cry, Wisteria looks up. "Mom!"

I'm really confused now and I don't think I'm going to have time to figure anything out. Asteria turns to me with a strange look in her eyes. Before I can react she places her fingers onto my temples. I go out like a lit wick that's been cut too short in a pool of melted candle wax.

I'm drowned in unconsciousness.

My thoughts are a jumble. I don't even know if I can be bothered to decide whether I'm awake or asleep. Maybe it doesn't matter. If I just stay asleep forever then I won't have to worry about being awake and dealing with the consequences of my nightmares.

And that does the trick. I realize that I must be dreaming if I'm thinking about being awake.

"Kaaaaaaaaate." A voice emanates into my unconsciousness. "Kaaaaaaaaaate... you... must... be... in... control..."

Control? Of what?

"Steer your dreams, Kaaaaaaate. Push out the nightmare elements. Bring reality into your nightmares..."

That's easier for whatever voice that is to say. I don't even know what it's talking about, let alone how to follow the spoken instructions.

Or do I?

Bring reality in?

Control the elements?

Is it possible? Could I control my dreams?

Concentrating hard, I get to the task at hand.

This entire time I've been feeling like I'm floating somewhere. The unrealistic landscape is blue and purple, if I were to put a name to the surrounding colors. There is a darkness inside my mind that I don't think I'll be able to escape. All around me is swirling madness. It's an endless clear night sky without a single star pinpointing the void.

"Kaaaaaaaaate. Be in Lakepoint..."

Lakepoint. Yes. That's a good star. My home town. The place where Titans live. The land where my best friend's home was so recently demolished. And it was destroyed by my boyfriend.

No. He's not my boyfriend. Thad isn't my boyfriend. He isn't the one I adore. Who is the guy I like? What is the name of the boy I'm really dating? Why can't I stop thinking about Thad?

Thad the fifty foot, scaly skinned monster who is the cause of the nightmares occurring in reality.

No again.

The nightmares are my fault.

No again and again.

The nightmares were brought to life by a girl, but I'm not the girl who made my dreams come true.

Wisteria.

A name close to that of her mother's.

Asteria.

That's the voice.

I know the sound of the voice who's trying to get through to me now. It's Asteria, goddess of dreams.

"Help me." My voice peeps through the dreamy gloom. "How do I control my nightmares?"

"You already are..."

Her voice has power to it. A power that seeps into my unconsciousness, making my thoughts congeal into a globby form of reality.

Suddenly, I'm in Lakepoint. Though the blue and purple starless sky is still swirling crazily above my head.

Thad is here. He's normal. He isn't fifty feet tall and his skin is smooth and silky, not green and scaly.

"Kate." He reaches out to me. We're both standing on Main Street, but everything is intact. There are no crushed buildings. No thrown cars or blasted out windows. "You're here."

I go to Thad. "Where are we?"

"I don't know, but I've been stuck here for a while. Do you think you could get us out of here?"

So Thad —the real Thad— has been in this weird dream place this whole time? "So you're not a fifty foot snake monster trying to eat all of the teenage girls in town?"

Thad's eyebrows shoot up questioningly on his forehead. "Not that I'm aware of, no."

"Sorry," I mumble. "You probably have no idea what's going on."

"And you do? Well that's a relief! I can't even move from this spot!"

"Really?" I look down at his feet. It looks like he's struggling to move, but the only resulting movement is a slight jittering of his legs. "Oh! You are stuck!"

"BRING HIM OUT, KATE. BRING IT ALL OUT."

"Who was that?" Thad balks at the loud emanating voice of Asteria. He looks up and all around.

I don't answer him, I'm too busy concentrating on what her voice is trying to say. "How?" I cry out. "How do I end this stupid dream?"

There is no answer from Asteria. There doesn't have to be as I've realized my own answer from my question.

I have to end this dream. It's my nightmare and it's time to wake up.

Thad has kept his hand outstretched towards me this entire time.

That's the key.

He's the answer.

Finally, I take his hand and the moment I do this wretched dream sifts into reality.

Now I know I'm awake.

Awake and being crushed.

Maybe it was a mistake to take Thad's hand, because I'm now being squeezed in his.

It's the fifty foot tall snake Thad and he's holding my entire body in his palm. Well, my waist anyway. Actually, either I'm expanding, or Thad's hand is shrinking.

Yes. That's definitely what's happening here.

Snake Thad gives out a deafening roar that winds down to a soft whisper. His form is shrinking. He's getting smaller. Eventually, he can no longer hold onto me and he drops me onto the ground. All the while he continues to shrink until he's once again at his normal height of six feet, with regular non-scaly skin.

"Thad!" I run to him and hug him tight. When I pull away he looks at me funny. I can tell he probably has a lot of questions.

"Kate!"

It's Shana. She's here and so is everyone else. All the Titans are still dressed in their glowing golden armour and it's really a sight to behold. The street, just before Main, is crowded with police cars, ambulances and firetrucks that all come swerving into the road at the same time.

The entire town has gathered to witness the chaos and I have a feeling it's going to be left up to me to explain everything.

*

Guess what I did?

I went to sleep.

You know how I said I'd never sleep 'perchance to dream' again?

Well, after everything I went through, I couldn't help myself. I just held up my hand, claimed amnesia and walked away from yesterday's gathering.

It's not that I'm uncaring. It's just the nightmare was finally over and I was tired. I mean really, really tired.

I walked home. Crawled into bed and slept until the next day, which is now. I'm sitting in Shana's intact kitchen as though no fifty foot tall monster snake boy had ever smashed through it in the first place.

It's amazing the magic that can unfold when an entire town of powerful Titan gods and goddesses combine forces. To fix a house. And buildings, and crashed up cars along Main Street. Also, the regular (non-god) townsfolk had all had their memories wiped. It was bad enough that the risk of Zeus finding out about this past week's incidents was in jeopardy, but if mere mortals went around blabbing there wouldn't be a soul or entity left in this world —or any other— who wasn't aware of what transpired.

"You know what I think?" Shana pops another corn chip into her mouth and talks through her crunchy food.

"I don't want to know." I've got my feet curled under me and we're both sitting at the kitchen table.

"I don't care. I'm gonna tell you anyway." Shana grins. "I think you totally have the hots for Thad and that's why he was in your waking dream."

Rolling my eyes, I don't say a word. I just knew my best friend would say something about my magical dream eventually.

"I don't have the hots for anyone... I mean, only Jason... I only have the hots for him."

"Then why didn't you tell him the truth?"

I scowl at Shana now. What's she getting at? Okay so I hadn't told Jason what happened when he texted and called me this morning.

"You know why I didn't say anything to Jason, it's because he's the son of Zeus, duh. Our parents don't want him finding out, remember?"

Now it's Shana's turn to scowl. She leans back in her chair and adds a *harrumph* of disgust for good measure. "That was a quick answer. How convenient."

Do I detect a hint of sarcasm in her reply? When she smirks at me it's confirmed. That was more like a huge wad of sarcasm.

Quickly, I change the subject. "I'm just here to find out what happened to Asteria and her crazy daughter. But if you don't want to tell me—"

"Hang on. I'll tell you. Just chill." Shana finishes off the packet of chips and gulps down her Coke. "You're not wrong about that girl being crazy. Yesterday she came out of nowhere with that Dillon guy. He looked like a zombie!"

"Oh yeah, you said he was dream walking. Being controlled by Wisteria!"

Shana nods. "Her mom, Asteria, told me later that she used Dillon to get Thad the giant out of the ground. It was insane, Kate!" She slams her hand dramatically down onto the table. "It's a good thing you showed up when you did, or this whole town would have been screwed."

"Were you serious when you said Asteria took her daughter to Tartarus?"

Shana raises her eyebrows. "Yep."

"Wow. I guess she was serious about punishing Wisteria. But does that mean she'll be grounded for like... a millennia?"

Shana shrugs her shoulders. "She deserves it. What a lunatic."

I guess Shana's right. From what I've heard no other kids in

Dillon's town discovered what Wisteria did. If there are Titans living there too though, it's only a matter of time before more demi-gods and demi-goddesses emerge.

Sighing loudly, I put my head into my hands and lean my elbows on the table.

"Do you wanna go back to bed again?" My best friend asks me.

I laugh a small chuckle and put down my hands. "No, I'm okay. There's just so much stuff to think about, you know?"

"Yeah, I know." Shana laughs. "My mom is some kind of earth goddess. Trust me, I know what you're thinking." She winks and suddenly the floor beneath my chair rumbles slightly.

"Did you just...?" My eyes bulge at my best friend.

She smiles wickedly.

"Shana!" I exclaim. "You're a demi-goddess!"

ABOUT THE AUTHOR

Suz Korb is an American British author living and writing in the midlands of England. Suz gets her story inspiration from anywhere and everywhere. In fact, one time she was staring out her livingroom window at a pine tree blowing in the wind. And thus her next novel character was born; a pilot who fights forest fires by strategically dumping loads of water from the air. Check out the author's website for updates on her next adventure.

SUZKORB.COM

Printed in Poland
by Amazon Fulfillment
Poland Sp. z o.o., Wrocław
24 May 2021